GROWING A NEW TAIL

To Adele, with thanks!

Lisa C Taylor

GROWING A NEW TAIL

ARLEN
HOUSE

Growing a New Tail

is published in 2015 by
ARLEN HOUSE
42 Grange Abbey Road
Baldoyle
Dublin 13
Ireland
Phone/Fax: 353 86 8207617
Email: arlenhouse@gmail.com
arlenhouse.blogspot.com

Distributed internationally by
SYRACUSE UNIVERSITY PRESS
621 Skytop Road, Suite 110
Syracuse, NY 13244–5290
Phone: 315–443–5534/Fax: 315–443–5545
Email: supress@syr.edu

978–1–85132–128–5, paperback

Typesetting by Arlen House

Front cover: *A Descent into Heather* by Robert Sparrow Jones
www.robertsparrowjones.com

Back cover: *House* by Janet Wormser
www.janetwormser.com

Cover design by Russ Taylor

Contents

For the journey
and for Russ who shares it

GROWING A NEW TAIL

VISIBLE WOUNDS

The place where they cut her throbbed with knowledge that skin acquires when it is sliced open, must grow a hood to heal. Standing in the lobby, Elsa wore layers, black turtleneck, jewel-coloured blouse, mauve over jacket. Her luggage remained untouched. Noon, she guessed by the rumble in her belly. Her name spoken quietly by the rapidly-blinking desk clerk. *Elsa.* Her room wasn't ready. Moving back from the line, she fretted about the luggage and wondered whether he would arrive by bus or car. The surgery only two days ago, it was early for her to travel, but her mother could not. The doctor said she could go, if she had to, *don't lift anything*.

A scarab, that's what it was, some kind of beetle tattoo on his wrist; she saw it when he bent down to pick up the leather briefcase and she remembered Gregor Samsa and *The Metamorphosis. We're all becoming something else.* What did he think of when he sat still for the needle to etch the perfect tiny insect into his flesh? His name was Patrick O'Rourke, P.X.O. on his briefcase. X as in Xavier or Malcolm X or anonymous, illiterate. X as in Xu or Xi. Now he met her gaze in the way strangers do when they recognise something of themselves in others. Not young but fortyish and trim. Well-dressed in a grey sport jacket, a black wool coat draped over his arm. He extended his hand, picked up her rolling luggage. Elsa followed him with buoyancy before her boots sank into the swirls of carpet. No words, just recognition. Either he was the dead woman's son or he was a stranger. He would take her to the funeral or he would rape and strangle her, careful not to soil his ironed white button-down.

His name was Patrick O'Rourke and his mother was a Vietnam War bride. Colonel James O'Rourke. *You're just supposed to fuck them; you're not supposed to marry them.* The Colonel's parents never accepted her. Her mother's Mahjongg partner and confidant. In Vietnam, he would have been a half-breed instead of a Harvard graduate and prominent lawyer. The tattoo elongated as he pulled her luggage down the empty hallway. Elsa said nothing. They were connected in the way everyone is connected to the people their families love. His mother brought her sister Lan over but her brother was in a shallow grave somewhere. Elsa's mother said the tragedies of others are difficult to fathom though the Holocaust obliterated Elsa's grandparents and Aunt Margaret.

Patrick X. O'Rourke lived in Cambridge, worked for the ACLU, taught part-time at Harvard. He had central heating, no wife. Elsa thought of her own failed two-year marriage to Will. *We're all becoming something else.* The site of her surgery throbbed. When did Patrick get the tattoo? Tattoos were like visible wounds.

'My room is ready. Why don't you store your luggage there?'

Patrick's voice had a slight nasal Boston accent and she thought momentarily of Ted Kennedy and all those other doomed Kennedys.

'Thanks'.

Elsa looked into the broad expanse of his face, rice paddies and heat. Perfect white teeth.

'Would you like to get some lunch before the funeral?'

The hollow feeling in her belly, body asserting its needs. The surgery only two days ago; she fasted beforehand, checked herself out of Brigham and Women's Hospital, took a taxi back to her two bedroom condo in Jamaica Plain. She remembered the Vicodin in her purse.

'Thanks. Yes'.

Patrick knew an Asian Fusion restaurant two blocks from the Hilton and Elsa almost forgot the funeral. Summer rolls, hot and sour soup. Was this similar to the food of his ancestors? Her ancestors ate heavy potato dishes with sour cream and overcooked tough cuts of meat. His name was Patrick O'Rourke and he had gone to Catholic School – St Mary's. Public school for Elsa, Britham High School and later the public university where she got a Master's in Social Work. *You work too hard for nothing*, her mother said. She helped place children in pre-adoptive homes. Some of them were Vietnamese.

They met as children, read comic books while their mothers played Mahjongg. A Vietnamese and a Jew. Linh O'Rourke was a war bride and her husband sacrificed everything to bring her to America. His parents never accepted her, shamed, Elsa's mother said, even when she converted to Catholicism. The priest accepted her, Patrick had said, but the family remained bitter until their death. But James O'Rourke loved her, taught her English, bought her a diamond ring and took her on trips to China, Ireland and Puerto Rico. She didn't want to go back to Vietnam. They were married fifty-one years, until his death at eighty. She was only seventy-three when she got breast cancer. Two years a widow.

Bette, Elsa's own mother was seventy-six and had a heart condition. *Go, Elsa. Go and pay my respects. Linh was my good friend.* She wanted to say no, couldn't say no. Her surgery only two days ago and there were moments when the pain reminded her of the ache she felt when Will left. He returned her to the single world as if she were a piece of furniture he didn't mean to order. *We're all becoming something else.*

Elsa wanted to ask Patrick about the tattoo but thought it rude. *You ask too many questions,* Will had told her. It moved when he ate his soup, drank his Thai ice tea. He had perfect teeth, smiled at her in a way that made her remember what it was like to want someone.

'My mother said you're a social worker. We don't live far from each other, you know'.

She knew. His name was Patrick X. O'Rourke and he lived in Cambridge. Outside the window of the restaurant, a light snow breathed its moth-like mist and coated the sidewalk, lingering on the hats and jackets of bustling people. All colours walked by; an orange pea coat, a brown fur jacket, royal blue wool. Elsa fingered her handmade green scarf.

'I work with families who can't have children'.

'I know. I've heard about you from my mother. She wanted us to be friends again'. He slowed down when he said the word *friend* so it sounded like an invitation. She thought of *friends with benefits.*

A Jew and a Catholic. A Vietnamese and a Caucasian. The lines are different here, she could see that. Will's avowed atheism had bothered her mother. *I don't care what he believes as long as he believes in something. It's arrogant to think there is nothing else.* She supposed it was arrogant. Will didn't believe in marriage either. No children and she was thirty-six. The surgery just two days ago and the incision hurt. She could still have children; the doctor said so.

'We should go. I need to get to the funeral home. Most of Mother's friends have died and there is so little family left. Your mother was like family'.

Outside the snow piled up like insulation, and Patrick took her hand. Her breath made little clouds that merged with the little clouds of his breath. The scarab was almost touching her. *We're all becoming something else.*

Elsa imagined scar tissue growing over her wound, new skin. Her body sloughed off the bad cells and in its place something strong and healthy would emerge.

The snow muted traffic noises as if the city slept under a blanket. They decided to walk the three blocks to the funeral home, the pressure of his hand guiding her. His name was Patrick O'Rourke. The funeral of his mother Linh brought her to New York, her luggage stowed in his room. She couldn't lift anything but she would be fine. The doctor said she could have children. Not a malignancy. Where they cut her, there would be a tiny half-moon scar, like an upside-down smile.

They arrived at a Victorian house, McCabe's Funeral Home, stately with gingerbread detailing like an elaborate wedding cake. Men in black wool coats parked cars. No crowd. Most of his mother's friends were dead. Someday Elsa's mother would die and Patrick would come to the tony suburb of Andover. She'd take him to her favourite French bistro. Her mother's family died in the Holocaust. So much death. It would be wrong not to believe in something, wrong not to try to carry on.

She found his card in her purse when she got back to her room. *Patrick X. O'Rourke, Public Interest Attorney/Legal Director, ACLU/211 Congress Street/Boston, MA,* a scribbled email on the back. He asked her to meet him for a drink later. She remembered the Vicodin. Where they cut her throbbed like a pulse. Eight o'clock. They would meet at Murphy's Pub. The Vicodin numbed but didn't quell the pain. Sixteen people at the funeral. Most of her friends were dead. *Elsa, Pay my respects. Linh was my good friend.* Patrick spoke of his mother's long braid, flower garden, tiger lillies and hyacinth. Bette Freeman and Linh

O'Rourke. Saturday afternoon Mahjongg. She would sneak downstairs and Linh would slip her a brownie. Linh and Bette smoked Pall Malls until they made a pact to quit. *So much death.*

The water in the shower felt warm, not hot. Where they cut her, an angry welt remained. The soap smelled like lilies. Elsa traded her black turtleneck for a rose-coloured blouse, loose skirt. She pulled a comb through her long hair, straight, *like an Asian,* Will once said. Dr Rosynski said she would be fine, could even have children someday. No malignancy. They would meet at Murphy's Pub and she would chat. His tattoo would stretch when he held the glass. Two diamond studs like chips of ice in her ears. His hand had touched her hand, and now there was a lace coverlet of snow outside. He had placed her luggage on the rack, rolling it quietly into her room after the funeral. Eight o'clock. *It would be wrong not to believe in something.* A Catholic and a Jew. He said he was a Buddhist, meditated daily. She believed in seasons, felt hopeful when the dogwood returned with its frilly blossoms.

His name was Patrick X. O'Rourke and she was Elsa Freeman. They would meet for a drink. His mother was a war bride. *You're just supposed to fuck them; you're not supposed to marry them.* She would order club soda and wait for a sign, an X like Xavier or anonymous but he was not anonymous. His card, a ticket or an invitation on her night table. They used to read comic books, *Spiderman* and *Archie.* He wore black-rimmed glasses then. Sometimes the past can seem like the future. *I want you to be happy,* her mother said before she left. *Go, and pay my respects to Patrick. He's a good son.* Happy was a word like chitchat or marriage. She never had a brother and her sister moved beyond the scope of her imagining. Linh wanted them to know each other. Skittering snowflakes outside of her window. Will left in late spring when Linh's lilies were beginning to open. She remembered the garden and his mother's long grey braid of hair. A Catholic and a Jew. Sometimes what you believe can change. He had a scarab on his right wrist that everyone could see when he picked up a pen, typed on his computer, texted on his phone. He was right-handed and his middle initial was X for the mark that was upon him, a visible wound, an upside-down smile or the memory of an uncle in a shallow grave, ancestors riding cattle cars to concentration camps. He was the son of her mother's friend or he was a stranger. They would meet for a drink or she would go to Murphy's Pub and find no one but the tired bartender.

She opened the door as if it were a book she was beginning to read. She opened the door as if the outside might get in, a mound of snow settling on the spotless carpet, around the framed photo of Times Square. Riding the elevator down, she felt a pulling and an ache. The doctor said she could have children. He was a Buddhist Catholic half-Vietnamese public interest attorney. She was Elsa Freeman, a Jewish believer in something, though she wasn't sure what it was, if it was shaped like a scarab, would settle or melt like ice.

FIVE PERCENT

I didn't like the tone of his voice, the way he told me to come down to the police station *straight away*. I almost hit a squirrel, just missed a row of decorative hedges because I was thinking about Eddy, his uneven teeth, the cowlick he tried to tame with a dab of my hair gel, and the dirty socks I found under the bed yesterday. The sun scorched overhead when I pulled into the last space. Wednesday morning and the police station parking lot was full.

A round-faced balding man opened the door for me as if he'd been standing there waiting. *Detective Tomas Underwood.* He stuck out his hand in the way men do when they forget that shaking hands is a mostly male ritual. I gripped his stubby fingers awkwardly, pumping them a few times.

'Don't worry, Miss Bolton. Most missing persons are located within forty eight hours'.

Why *persons* not *people*? When had Eddy become a forensic cliché? Were the newly missing simply lost like a kitten? I thought of the arborist who rescued Minx from our towering hemlock tree when I was seventeen.

Handsome in the way of some labourers, my hand grazed his as he passed me the cat. My mother had her put down two months later, said she wasn't trainable. *Just a bad pet all around.*

Detective Underwood handed me a yellow legal pad and a pen like computers weren't yet invented, told me to recreate everything from last night. *In longhand. Leave nothing out.* But I omitted the bottle of Merlot we split, the lovemaking that left a path of clothing from the kitchen to the bedroom, and the kiss.

I didn't tell him how we once planned to move in together, put in some raised beds for a vegetable garden, get a Weber grill for barbeques; maybe buy one of those Craftsman style homes in the better section of town near enough to our jobs but away from the highway noise. None of it mattered now. What difference did it make that Eddy bought me a bouquet of gaudy dahlias last week for no reason, texted me throughout the workday?

5:00 – Ate dinner. Chicken and mushroom risotto. Eddy made a salad. We had fruit and cheese later, watched television, *CSI Miami.*

10:00 – Went to bed. Eddy had to be up early because it was his day to open the clinic. Set the alarm for 5:30 so we'd have time to go to the gym.

6:30 – Went to gym in separate cars. He swims laps and I lift weights and run.

7:45 – Left gym, stopped for coffee.

8:05 – Eddy texted me, said *Have a good day, luv* with one of those smiley-face icons, the one with the wink (I showed him the text, the last one I'd gotten from Eddy).

10:00 – Clinic called, asked if I'd seen Eddy. I told them we were at the gym together and I'd assumed he headed straight for work to open the clinic. His supervisor, Dr. Metcalf, said he never showed up.

After Eddy disappeared, his mother, Sofia, brother, Franco, and his best friend, J.L. called me in succession. None of them had heard from him. I tried to keep a routine. On Saturday, I used my key to retrieve the favourite cashmere sweater I'd left draped over his couch. The police had been through his apartment, confiscated his laptop and iPad and left a mess of open drawers, linens and clothes in a heap on the floor.

Eddy would never cheat on me. Sometimes I thought I didn't deserve him. We started dating nine months ago after I interviewed him for an article on local clinics offering a percentage of their care *gratis* for the poor. Eddy stared at my breasts during the interview – not subtly like some men do, pretending to be looking over your shoulder or out the window, full on staring like they weren't real or something. I even glanced down to check my buttons. If he hadn't invited me for a proper date at a Zagat rated restaurant that would have been the end of it. I figured the dude owed me for all that ogling. Eddy didn't try to kiss me that night, just gave me a friendly hug and a peck on the cheek. I thought I'd hit the fucking lottery.

His Jeep was found parked in a wooded area near my apartment, keys still in the ignition, navy blue sports coat in the back seat, workout clothes in a gym bag in the trunk. *No evidence of foul play.*

Mama tried to cheer me up.

'Maybe he had a wife in another state or he wasn't an American and he got deported'.

No. Eddy Ventura was Brooklyn born and raised. Sofia, his Italian born mother could attest to that. We travelled to Brooklyn for Easter last year and I swear she slaughtered a whole pig for the feast. I'd never seen anything like it and my mama isn't skimpy on food. Sofia liked me, nagged Eddy to propose.

'Eddy, Jodie's a good girl. Why don't you settle down? You waiting for royalty or what?'

Eddy never answered, just grinned his lopsided grin, the one that showed the gap between his crooked front teeth that he could afford to fix but it wasn't a priority.

Mama told me, 'It's a curse to be a pretty woman. Great to be smart as a whip, win a scholarship to one of the Ivies. Plain girls get left alone. You got the smart, Jodie but not the plain. Lecherous fools, the lot of them. It's the Ninety-Five Percent Rule. Only five percent of men you'll meet are worth a damn'.

Though I take issue with Mama on everything from my dead no-good father to the incident with Minx, I've remembered this. I didn't need to be anyone's trophy girlfriend.

Eddy and I had discussed marriage but neither of us felt ready. If he had any secrets, I never heard about them, and he didn't ask me about my past. Ok by me. I've never understood that sordid need to tell all. He was the kind of guy who put the toilet seat down, rinsed out the sink after shaving, even baked a cake from scratch for my birthday, sprinkled with coconut and shaved chocolate, though I had to eat around the coconut.

On that last night, we made mad love, giggling as we moved from room to room in my tiny apartment. Until he tried to kiss me. I cannot stand being kissed, except the chaste close-mouthed kind relatives give at weddings and funerals. Even though he knew I didn't like it, Eddy was all about open-mouthed kisses with lots of tongue.

When Eddy kissed me, something opened up inside of me. I pulled away and locked myself in the bathroom, ignored the incessant pounding on the door.

'C'mon Jo. Don't be such a baby'.

Some days it's possible to open a door and the person you most want to see will be standing there. But it's just as easy to wake up in the middle of the night with your father dressed in plaid pajamas, reeking of gin.

It's best to learn this at home, Jo-Jo. You'll thank me someday.

A week later, I got the voicemail. At the station Detective Underwood told me the story of Dr Eddy Ventura, one of the five percent of faithful men in the world, the same man who volunteered for *Doctors without Borders*, never got so much as a parking ticket and could make a perfect omelette, cheese melted on the inside, edges fully cooked.

'A body was found in upstate New York. Actually two, a man and a woman. No positive identification yet but we suspect that Eddy may have been in that region visiting his daughter so we're examining all of the possibilities'.

'Daughter?'

Bile rose in my throat. I swallowed hard. They would have the identification back tomorrow but I knew what I knew.

When I got to J.L'.s house, he looked as if he hadn't groomed himself in days, the circles under his eyes dark as bruises. After a perfunctory hug, he held the door open and I could see a stricken Sofia on the couch.

'Sit down', J.L. motioned to a chair piled with newspapers and biker magazines. An open pizza box with what looked like day old pizza sat on the coffee table along with a list of names and a pencil crossing them out. I was third on the list.

'I'm no good at this sort of thing', J.L. said.

'Our Eddy is dead, Jodie. Our Eddy is dead. What kind of monster would do a thing like this?'

'We don't know for sure, Sofia. They don't have a positive identification'.

'I *know*, Jodie. I can feel it'. She thumped on her chest, pushing aside her lawn-coloured silk scarf.

Outside the wind kicked up. Sofia sat up straight and adjusted her scarf knot when something slammed against the front window.

'I told Eddy that woman was bad news. In rehab for drugs, tattooed. My Eddy, he finally listened, broke up with her. I didn't even know about the child'. Sofia put her face in her hands, sobbing.

J.L. shrugged it off. 'No crime to have a daughter. Everyone has a past'.

I hadn't kissed Eddy that night until he pushed the issue, backed me against the kitchen wall so hard, my Old Town vintage clock, the one with Roman numerals, clattered to the floor, glass face in little shards all over the linoleum. I can still feel the scratchiness of the plaster wall against my back and Eddy's arms pinning me, hard muscles from all those freestyle laps at the pool.

When they called to tell us that the body wasn't Eddy's but a drifter's, I didn't care if the other body was his old girlfriend or not. Still no sign of Eddy. Sofia and Franco took the morning train to meet the child. J.L. invited me over for beer and pizza. I didn't have a better offer.

All day long I stared at my computer screen, images of that last night nagging at me. A leer and a kiss I didn't want to give, even when he persisted.

C'mon Jo-Jo, how about some loving?

Don't call me that Eddy.

Oh Jo-Jo, just one little kiss. C'mon baby, show me you love me.

When I close my eyes, I can make people disappear.

DENTS AND RUTS

They did it deliberately, uprooting the violets with their motorcycles, leaving clumps of dirt the size of hockey pucks. Before they came along, Doone's Ridge looked like one of those bucolic New England destinations advertised in a travel magazine. Wildflowers dotted the hillside in spring, and on clear days Jerry could see the white roof of the Plainville fire station and Schofield's Farm with its grazing calves and lambs. He'd bring an oilcloth to sit upon while he looked out clear to the border town, the place Kiley said they could never afford to live.

The Marshfield Preservation League volunteer told him that Doone's Ridge belonged to everyone, even the scumbags who smoked weed and left cigarette butts and Budweiser cans along the grassy promontory.

Kiley didn't take any of it seriously.

'Jeez, Jerry. They're just kids. Didn't you do stupid crap when you were that age or were you born using a silicone sleeve to protect your coffee cup?'

The damn sleeve again. She'd made fun of him when he bought it, said it was another one of his neurotic habits like the blue latex gloves for washing dishes, the antibacterial hand sanitiser he carried with him in a pocket-sized dispenser or the way he insisted on changing the sheets every other day because of dust mites and skin.

'Do you know how much skin and hair we shed? It's like sleeping in a graveyard of dead cells', Jerry had told her.

'Who gives a damn about skin, hair, or anything else we lose? If you lose a finger in your sleep or your penis drops off, that would be something to worry about'.

He didn't mind that his wife had the constitution of a lumberjack; it made him feel safer. *Built like a brick shithouse.* Nearly six feet tall barefoot, she had forty-inch hips and a forty-two inch bust, but no fat on her. Solid, like a structure that would be intact in seventy or eighty years. He knew she'd outlive him and told her so regularly.

'That's because you worry about the guy who has to clean up spilled popcorn at the movie theatre and what they do with the drinks they make by mistake at Starbucks'.

Still it annoyed him that she regularly took her phone into the bathroom with her and wouldn't let him wipe it down with disinfectant afterward. He had rubbed off most of his right eyebrow, ground his teeth at night and now his bottom teeth were little stubs. Dr Parmelee gave him an appliance but he knew it was toxic to have something in his mouth all night. What if the plastic had that BPA in it? He'd talked Kiley out of using microwavable plastic for just that reason.

'Stuff leaches out of it, you know. Bad hormone mimicking stuff. It's the same with that appliance'.

'Shit is everywhere, Jerry. We're breathing it and eating it. Might as well have a beer and watch a game'.

'I'm serious. I can't put that thing in my mouth and suck on it all night'.

'No one is asking you to suck on it, just protect what little teeth you have left. Dentures are not an attractive option for a thirty-five year old, you know'.

But the appliance jiggled in his mouth and tasted like a balloon.

Sedatives gave him a headache and made him fuzzy the next day. Not a good thing for an electrician. Once he nearly electrocuted himself, forgetting the circuit breaker before he wriggled into a customer's crawl space to wire for an attic fan.

On Saturday, Kiley suggested the Citizens of Marshfield meeting.

'You have to go through the right channels if you want to change something. There's a meeting today at the town hall'.

She was usually right. In her job as a police officer, she erred on the side of safety. Anyone in trouble would want her around because she didn't overreact even when Jerry thought she should. She could be ready for a weekend in ten minutes flat, pulling a comb through her hair and rolling on a little deodorant. He'd have to go through the bags at least three times in case he'd forgotten to pack the spare sheet, mattress cover and extra pairs of briefs. Now they just stayed home or Kiley visited her elderly aunt who lived in one of those retirement homes that smelled like urine and bleach.

Kiley pulled out her mirror, applied some lipstick. Jerry kissed her cheek. He would clean off his lips later with wet wipes he kept in the glove box.

By the time he got to the highway, torrential rain, the kind that transforms a road into a stream, began to fall. Cars were pulling over in the breakdown lane. A grey Honda hydroplaned and skidded into the guardrail. This was Kiley's fault for suggesting he turn anger into activism. Why didn't she warn him about the weather? She was always checking her smartphone. The Concerned

Citizens of Marshfield didn't care about Doone's Ridge or the little trail he made, relocating earthworms and hacking away at poison ivy.

Jerry noticed an oversized red pick-up truck pulled over. When he reached for the other eyebrow, the one he hadn't yet rubbed off, though it was getting thin, he jostled his glasses. Later he would say he wasn't sure when the spin happened or how he knew to straighten the wheel, especially because he could barely see anything with his glasses askew. The passenger side of his Ford Focus slammed into the pick-up and Jerry's car came to a grinding halt. A dented cab door opened, and a tall skinny man wearing a bright yellow slicker climbed down. The first thing that went through Jerry's mind was that a man that tall shouldn't wear yellow. Then the man pounded his leather-gloved fist on Jerry's window, stared at him with bloodshot eyes.

'Didn't you see my truck? It's red, for fuck's sake. You slammed into my truck, asshole'.

'I'm sorry, sir. The rain'. Jerry waved his hand at the torrent.

'Rain, my ass. It's called driving. You move to the breakdown lane if you can't drive, Dickhead. This is going to cost you big time. I just had her detailed'.

By then a police officer had pulled over, blue lights flashing.

The dent on the truck looked miniscule compared to the side of Jerry's car. *This is going to cost you big-time* was all Jerry could think of. He'd already taken out a home equity loan without telling Kiley because he had to replace the couch and mattress since it had been three years and he couldn't bear the thought of the millions of dust mites that had taken up residence. He'd seen a magnified picture of mites and they looked a lot like crabs or lobsters. The thought of something with tiny pinchers lurking in his furniture was unbearable.

$175.00 was the amount of the fine plus he had to exchange insurance information with Wayne Lambert, a telephone pole of a man in a silly raincoat who kept punching the side of his smashed up car with a fist.

Finally Jerry headed home, composing stories that he could tell Kiley – a truck skidded into his car (she'd be concerned, want him to go to the Emergency Room to get checked out); he hydroplaned and hit a tree (shouldn't have gone out in such bad weather); someone hit him in the parking lot when he stopped to get coffee (hit and run). The hydroplane story seemed plausible and she'd feel guilty that she allowed him out in such a storm. Sometimes she'd make cookies when she felt guilty – warm and chocolately cookies.

When he saw the police car parked in his driveway, Jerry reached for his somewhat intact eyebrow. The rain had stopped, leaving the air fresh smelling, a citrus light peeking through. The distant hum of dirt bikes on the ridge intensified like a swarm of mosquitoes. Jerry hurried to the back door.

Murray Snyder had his arm around Kiley's shoulder. Sergeant Murray Snyder, a man who surpassed Kiley in stature. As soon as Jerry opened the door, Murray removed his arm, stepped back, bumping into the centre island.

'Hey, man. How ya doin' Jerry?' Murray shoved his enormous hand in an equally large pocket and backed up a few steps. 'Just talking to Kiley about the patrols we gotta do now that we're zeroing in on a drug bust'.

'What drug bust?' Had Kiley mentioned Murray coming over? Wiping up something with a sponge, one hand wrapped around a beer can, Kiley tipped the can, pouring golden liquid down the drain. That reminded Jerry that he had to pee, and he headed down the hall with Kiley close behind him. Then he saw the rumpled bed, big dents from big people. Big people rolling around on the sheets he was going to change tonight. Jerry reached instinctively for his left eyebrow, before he stopped, swallowed and straightened up. He put on the face he used when he was installing someone's track lighting or wiring their house for a generator, ignoring the layer of dust or the smell of cat pee. *Electrician brain*, he called it, a necessary detachment from other people and their messes. He'd wash his hands with pocket hand sanitizer, soak his tools in alcohol later but in the meantime, he'd get out his drill and screwdriver and do a proper job of it.

'Don't jump to conclusions, Jerry. It's not what it seems'. Kiley followed his gaze, her mouth flat and long like an earthworm.

Jerry forgot his bladder, pulled himself up to full height, still short of Kiley's.

'Rainy day so I got sleepy. Murray dropped by to discuss our plans to catch those drug dealers'. Kiley moved one bare foot in front of the other, bending her big toe so it made a swishing noise on the wood floor. She wasn't even wearing socks.

'Sure. I understand. I was daydreaming when I hit a big-ass truck and totalled the Ford. I'm awake now though'. Jerry held the word *now* for a beat, elongating the O.

'Hey, Jerry. Calm down. Nothing happened, man'. Murray's enormous feet clomped down the hallway. His hand still held the mug of beer, and the other hand was looking for a place to go. Jerry didn't want to think about the other places that hand had been.

'Ok, man. I'm leaving'. Murray hightailed it back to the kitchen with Kiley and Jerry close behind him. Plunking his mug in the sink, he opened the door, screeches and whimpers of dirt bikes filling the room. Kiley squirted blue liquid in the dishpan, swished the sponge inside the mug, the tiny bubbles settling like blisters on her arms and hands. Skin cells, pollen and bits of dirt danced in the sunbeam from the skylight over the sink.

Jerry sagged against the soapstone counter, counted silently to five hundred before opening the screen door. In his dented car, he pushed back the seat until he was almost prone. After the last biker's nasal whine had faded, crickets and peepers took over. Under the porch light, the driveway blended into the yard and beyond, the path to Doone's Ridge stretched out like a grey-purple ribbon. Head in his hands, Jerry opened his mouth but no sound came out, just germs and bits of saliva, the disgusting mechanics of breathing. Kiley had turned off the outside lamp, the light in the bedroom now golden against the blinds. He imagined her blue-striped nightshirt, the one with buttons he liked to undo, her warm bulk and sleepy murmurings. As he blew out air, it seemed as if the skin in his mouth was breaking down, bits of him disintegrating, carried off into the soundless night.

Monuments

He never blamed me outright but asked over and over *didn't you see the truck?* I see it in my dreams. It is behind me in the grocery store, in back of the classroom when I teach. The truck is parked outside when I'm at my damn book group. Yeah, Luke. I see the fucking truck. It won't bring Serena back.

He didn't even stop. A rabbit or a squirrel, he thought. I used to call her Bunny. Serena died on a perfect blue sky morning in mid-November. Dried leaves and road dust. I'll never have another child and I'll never love anyone as much as I loved Serena. Wyatt knows this. Luke does too, though I pretend it's my secret. He stopped brushing my hair, massaging my shoulders, started staying late at his office. When I spotted him in Delarosa's Restaurant, an arm draped around the shoulder of a copper-skinned woman, I brushed right past them. Pretending is a game that younger couples play. I lost her ten years ago today, a day when fair weather clouds were bloated enough to swallow airplanes.

It's my one teaching day so I get dressed, poke through my top drawer until I find the blue glass bead Serena gave me for Mother's Day when she was five. I slip it into the pocket of my black silk blazer. That day Serena named all the things that were the same colour: robin's eggs, her eyes, the blue part of the stained glass window in the Episcopal Church, Wyatt's matchbox car, and the pillow Grandma Bridget made her. Perhaps that's why we have children.

A long time ago, I planned to be an academic, never have to get a 'real' job out there in the less forgiving world. Steeping myself in the world of ideas and imagination sounded perfect. Luke and I used to spend hours in coffee shops on campus listening to snippets of conversation.

Did you see the ass on her and she's a professor.

An example of negative capability. Americano?

You could write a novel about the dramas that unfold. People break up, fall in love, swear off drugs, alcohol, discover Rilke or Shakespeare or master quadratic equations.

When they found the driver, it made no difference. Duane Anderson, III, a part-time truck driver, late to an interview for a security guard job. He had three children and no money. Negligent homicide and leaving the scene of an accident. Eight years, suspended after five. It's true what they say about revenge; you think you want it, that somehow it will make you feel better but it doesn't. He didn't see her, was thinking about the interview and how desperately he needed that job. His own daughter one year younger than Serena, a sweet-faced little girl whose photo he pulled out on the witness stand. She lost her Daddy for five years. Where's the justice in any of it? I wanted to hate him, didn't hate him. The world just felt like a shitty place.

When the trial ended Duane Anderson III sent me a letter.

I'm sorry.
I wish I could bring back yur little girl.
I think about it evry day.
Yours Truly,
Duane Anderson III

Thank you, Mr Anderson. It comforted me to know that the barely literate man who ran over my daughter was repentant.

'I didn't want you to get upset', Luke told me when I found the letter hidden under a pile of newspapers I was taking to the recycling bin.

'Fucking brilliant'.

I was glad it haunted Duane, hoped it followed him to his grave, poor bastard.

Eight months after Serena died, I took off my wedding ring. It's in my jewellery box, which I suppose is foolish because it would be the first thing to be stolen if someone broke into our house. *Officer, it was a yellow gold band of channel-set diamonds.* I don't think Luke even noticed. Teaching and screwing graduate students took up a lot of his time.

Definition of a good husband, according to Google:

Someone who wants to grow old with you. (Define 'old')

Someone who is generally happy alongside you no matter what happens. (Define 'happy')

Someone who loves you for who you are, your unique personality and lifestyle. (Define 'love')

The parenthetical comments are mine. I like the last one because it is so inclusive. And the growing old one. Ted Beemer, long married, seemingly loyal and contented until he took up with a twenty-something. Ted wasn't an academic. He was our mechanic. He moved in with Veronica, Vanessa, Victoria ... whatever the hell her name was ... blissful for maybe four months before she figured out that a fifty-nine year-old wasn't that exciting. What did he do? He talked Kate into taking him back. Not me. I wouldn't take Luke back. I'd have sold the house by the time he asked.

Was Duane Anderson III faithful to his wife? Sometimes I think of the sad-eyed woman in the courtroom day after day. Did she lie next to him at night? Did they have another child? Duane has been free for years now. I don't doubt that he was a model prisoner.

When I get home from class, Luke is sipping a gin and tonic. My mobile phone vibrates on the counter where I laid it down along with my keys and purse. Luke sidles up and hands it to me. He's doing the sidestep thing I used to think was so sexy. One day, intensified by the worse heat wave in years, he sidestepped through the back door of my rental house so quietly that I jumped when his hands encircled my waist, my hands submerged in soapy water.

'Mine', he said, pulling me toward the bedroom, just a mattress on the floor. I smelled like Joy dish soap mixed with sweat. No curtains on the windows, which were ground floor and open.

'Someone will see us', I protested as he unhooked my bra with one deft move. I could hear Mr Van Dorsen's lawnmower next door, wondered when the post would arrive.

'Shhhh'. He pushed me down on the double bed tucked in neatly with the daisy-patterned sheets of my childhood. As we sunk down, he twisted off his jeans, boxers, unzipped my denim skirt.

'I have to finish the dishes', I said weakly. If this were the last day of the world, an apocalypse, I'd want to fall back on that bed again, with its green velvet pillow, Indian bedspread in a pile on the floor, package of birth control pills on the bedside next to a pipe filled with weed. Midday; classes in an hour or so but we couldn't wait. In that moment, I was Joyce's Molly Bloom. *His heart was going like mad and yes I said yes I will yes.* There, on the patterned sheets, he pushed his way inside of me and I let him, as I would again, even knowing what I know. That is the great human tragedy, that we're imbeciles groggy with lust, bitches mounted in the park. Desire churns and we go forward as I did all those years ago, my panties sticky through Statistics and Renaissance Literature.

Our freshman-in-college son Wyatt is on the phone.

He tells me about his new girlfriend Belle. *She's not white.* I don't care. *She's from Rwanda.* Genocide. *Her family left before the killing in 1994. She was actually born here.* Explains the 'Belle' I think. *She speaks English, French, and Kinyarwanda, the language of Rwanda.* I didn't know that.

I reassure him that we're fine with Belle-from-another-place and her chocolate-coloured skin. Wyatt tells me he likes Web Design, doesn't like English Composition. Belle is teaching him some words in Kinyarwanda. She's a vegetarian and will dine with us on Saturday. Luke is watching me as if to memorize how to talk to our son. I tell him she's vegetarian and he looks relieved. 'Not bad to be vegetarian', he says. Even professors are vegetarian. Wyatt, our son who spent every weekend in high school playing computer games, has a girlfriend. We smile at each other.

Luke's seminal work on Shakespeare's antiheroes garnered a fellowship in England for the next academic year though I've made no commitment to join him nor do I want to disrupt Wyatt's studies.

Luke fixes another drink, asks me if I want to go out for Thai food so we can discuss England. The late afternoon sun sends flecks of light that seem to chase each other on our beige walls. What is the weather like in Britain? Will there be endless banter with imported wives and academics? I remember our early dinner parties with Dr and Mrs So and So or Dr and Dr So and So. Chaucer and Rashi. Shakespeare and the beginning of Luke's interest in tragic heroes like Macbeth. Lady Macbeth questioning his manliness to egg him on to commit murder.

What beast wasn't then
That made you break this enterprise to me?
When you durst do it, then you were a man;
And to be more than what you were, you would
Be so much more the man ...

Hamlet, Othello, Shylock. Men with questionable morals. Lucas P. Calvano, tenured professor and philanderer. Part-time husband and father. My own research on the secret and sacred texts, the bawdy writing of the ancients, rebellions and taboos that now languished in unopened files on my computer. *What hangs at a man's thigh and wants to poke at the hole it's often poked at before? Answer: A key.* How little we've progressed.

At first I had pharmaceuticals. Prozac and Zoloft. Elevate those serotonin levels. Chemicals can rearrange the brain that became altered when I retrieved a blood-spattered Barney lunchbox from the road. The problem was, I *wanted* this pain. It was my monument to Serena, better than the cold granite marker Luke put in our garden next to a yellow rose bush. Serena Joy Calvano, beloved sister and daughter. 16 May 1998 – 7 November 2004. A psychologist had told him that a physical marker would give me a place where I could sit and talk to her. I knew she wasn't there, her ashes scattered in the ocean off Cape Cod on a boat ride we took that summer.

'I don't like how the drugs make me feel', I told Luke after I tapered off of them months later. He pursed his lips. *Ding!* Wrong answer.

'Tessie. I'm worried about you'. His hand had snaked across the table. I remember jerking my hand back. I wasn't three. Even Serena at six was smarter than this.

'Maybe fucking graduate students is your way of coping but this is my life'.

'What is your life like now?'

No right answer and *ding!* I lost again. Down to teaching one class and going to the gym because my body was an ugly worm. My only social commitment was book group once a month.

Now we sit at a lacquered table, sipping Thai ice teas, swirling cream in the fluted glasses of liquid the colour of an August sunrise.

'Why should I go?'

Luke fidgets with the maroon napkin, takes another draw on the iced tea.

'I can't stagnate waiting for you to heal and I had this crazy thought that maybe this would be good for you, a new start'.

The server brings spring rolls with peanut sauce. They look like they're made with human skin.

'Heal? Losing my only daughter wasn't an illness'.

'Our daughter', he says.

'What I am supposed to do when you start sleeping around again?'

Luke stares at me, the mole under his left eye suddenly looking like a bug. He's handsome still, greying with little stitched lines at the corners of his eyes. He needs a shave. When we were dating, he shaved two times a day so his face wouldn't abrade me when we kissed. I loved his soft lips and his tongue imitating the act we were moving toward, the one I fell into two days ago, unwittingly. Now his eyes narrow and his lips are a thin line of disapproval.

'Tyra was a long time ago. I was trying to fill the gap left when Serena died. She was my baby, my little girl, eeny beenie Serenie'. Luke's eyes fill and I put my hand on his.

'Nothing could have prepared me. Plus I blamed you. God, I ran the scenario through my head hundreds of times. I knew you would have done the same thing if I had been the one waiting with her that day. Then I realised I probably would have turned to say hello to Diane as well. It took about three years to come to that and maybe another two to forgive you and accept that sometimes horrible things just happen. So many victims, don't you see? We have a chance. And for the record, I never slept with anyone else after Tyra. She moved out of the country and I threw myself into my research, hoping you'd do the same'.

'I guess I handle grief differently'.

'I know that now. Come to England with me'.

He knows I hate Northbrook. From the spider plants I kill to the tasteful draperies and groomed lawns, it has never felt like home. We don't entertain. It is a home for a family, which we haven't been in ten years.

I dip a spring roll in peanut sauce, take a bite and offer one to Luke. He bites into it with gusto, like he's a man of many appetites.

'Ok'. I say, as if saying it will make it real. One hand wrapped around the glass, the other lifeless on my lap, I am disconnected from my body.

I think of cucumber sandwiches and high tea, crossing the same ocean that swallowed Serena's ashes, the wind kicking up a grey cloud until fine dust dissipated on green waves. The three of us held hands that day, swaying and slightly nauseous with the tide.

Luke read an excerpt from *Winnie-the-Pooh*:

> *You are braver than you believe, stronger than you seem, and smarter than you think but the most important thing is ... even if we're apart, I'll always be with you.*

I remember thinking that it was a better thing to say than some religious drivel about being too good for this world or Serena becoming God's littlest angel.

A friend who wasn't a friend anymore told me she was in a better place. I walked out of the restaurant that day. There will never be a reason for tragedy, only the pain that makes a home in the body, manifesting itself during a television commercial where a little girl is ecstatic that her mother is coping with seasonal allergies, or in the park when a small blonde girl whispers something to her mother, both of them smiling and unaware that I am standing by the swings about to fall apart.

Under the table, I press my solar plexus hard enough to feel a twinge, breathe deeply into my diaphragm until she's there again, asking for something I denied her. Luke smiles, raises his glass of tangerine-hued tea and we clink glasses to the ocean we'll cross, flawed heroes and, of course, our daughter.

Narrow Paths Somewhere

Fiona awakened certain that the boy was alive. It came to her in a dream that added details like a book builds its plot from page to page. The groomed neighbourhood, boxy houses and a mailbox with a rusty hinge, room like the den of an animal, dank and feral. She could see Joey's hollow eyes, spindly arms. He disappeared on a sunny October day, one minute outside kicking a soccer ball and the next minute gone. Runaway, neighbours suspected. They had heard his parents arguing night after night, were sure that Ferd was drinking again. Search parties were organised, dogs brought in, given an old shirt of his to sniff. No leads. Salt Isle Grange took up a collection, and offered a $10,000 reward for information leading to an arrest or his safe return. October stretched into November and the winds were settling over Salt Isle. Everyone was thinking of that poor boy, with most folks assuming he was long dead, maybe at the bottom of the river by Arthur's Pass. No one wanted to talk about it but blue ribbons were tied on doors, mail posts and telephone poles, since blue was his favourite colour.

She called in sick to work then dialled the Salt Isle Police Department.

'Hi Bill. Fiona, here'.

'What can I do for you?' A golfing friend of Eamon's, he'd been over the house for a cookout with his wife and twin sons.

'Joey Mullen. Has he been found yet?' A blue jay hovered over the dog's bowl, pecking at the kibble Clark hadn't yet eaten.

'Ah, Fiona. Sad story. Hate to say it but we're losing hope. Every day that goes by makes it less likely poor Joey will be found alive'.

'I think he's in Louisiana. I jotted down the address: 345 Jefferson Terrace in Arcadia, Louisiana. Grey bungalow with old-fashioned shutters. There's a wooden swing hanging from a tree in the front yard. That's all I can tell you but please check it out. I'm quite sure that's the house. There's a small room with concrete floors, maybe in the basement'.

'How do you know?'

'I had a dream about it'.

'A dream, Fiona. You expect me to call the department in Louisiana and tell them someone in New Hampshire had a dream about a missing boy?'

'Please. I feel certain. I can't tell you how'. Fiona knocked on the kitchen window in an attempt to startle the jay.

'Ok, Fiona. Because I know you and all that, I'll give a shout to the boys in Louisiana'.

'Will you call me back and let me know?'

'You can be sure if this comes to anything but embarrassment, I'll call you straightaway'.

Fiona hung up the phone and went back to bed to see if the dream would return to her but it was gone. After giving Clark more food and walking him in the damp drizzle, running a load of laundry, and answering emails, she made herself a cup of tea, scooped in two teaspoons of sugar, added milk. Then the phone rang.

'Jesus, Mary, and Joseph, Fiona. You've got to tell me how you knew about the Mullen boy. I called the chief there. Damned if he didn't go to that address and this well-dressed man, kind of looked like a businessman he said, answered the door. The chief said he felt downright foolish, questioning a man who looked like a good citizen and all. Then he heard pounding. The man wouldn't let him in so he got a warrant, called for backup. When the others got there they stormed the house, found little Joey all bruised and battered in this horrible room next to the furnace. Joey's alive, thanks to you. Like *Silence of the Lambs* or something, I swear. Joey's in the county hospital, abused but alive. Amazing, Fiona. You've got a gift or something. How did you know?'

'I don't know. It was a dream. I'd be grateful if you didn't mention this to Eamon'.

'You know, there's $10,000 put up in reward money. That's yours, Fiona. I understand. Marriage is complicated. Sometimes less is more, if you know what I mean'.

'Thank you. I hope Joey will be ok'.

Fiona wondered if anyone was ever ok or if most people just faked it, pulling on the uniforms of their professions, sitting across tables from people legally bound to them. Last week Eamon said the chicken was tough, suggested they go out to dinner but Fiona ate hers, rose silently to load the dishwasher. Perfectly good chicken, bought from the butcher because Eamon didn't trust supermarkets. He had put his hand on her waist while she was washing up but she wriggled away, wrapped up his untouched portion.

The surprise of spring after a long winter festooned the trees with apple and cherry blossoms. Two of her patients had died, not unexpectedly but still, death seemed like a country she'd someday visit, one of those alternately hostile places where it wasn't safe to walk at night and women moved in groups like a train. When Eamon told her about the stillborn boy he delivered, Fiona called their college son, Mark just to hear his voice. She didn't tell him she was thinking about how he used to bat at a mobile in his crib and murmur gibberish that both reassured and amazed her.

Salt Isle was not a place of much drama. Most of the time teenagers throwing eggs at a house on Halloween, or an occasional robbery covered the front page of the local paper. The case of young Joey was the biggest thing that had happened in decades, but horror didn't always announce itself. Sometimes it just appeared, like her father in the wing chair, the hot smell of gunpowder, side of his head blown away like a paper maché puppet. She had been looking for a grocery bag to make a book cover, thought he was sleeping.

When she went to bed, Eamon grunted, rolled over. Exhausted from consecutive late nights, he barely stirred. Babies were born when they wanted to be born and spring, for whatever reason, was always a busy season for obstetricians. After the stillbirth and an emergency Caesarean last week at two am, it was hard for her to expect an uninterrupted night's sleep. But tonight, there were no calls, just a dream.

Water. A lake or maybe a pond. Lush and mature trees all around and a well-groomed lawn, golf course short. Two-storey brick house with Doric columns in the front and a Palladian window. Early 1800s, she guessed. Fiona could see a boxer running around in circles and the little white flags close to the ground that indicated an electric dog fence. 16 Hydrangea Lane, Williamstown, Massachusetts. Fiona had been to Boston and Sturbridge but not to Williamstown. She got up quietly, jotted down the address. The computer was downstairs so she tiptoed down the stairs and Googled the news in Williamstown.

Popular Teen Missing
Seventeen-year-old Jessica Hemphill-Morehead was reported missing on Tuesday after a school trip to nearby Tanglewood. Anyone with information is urged to call the Williamstown Police Department.

Three am but time might make a difference like it did for Joey. She picked up the phone.

After she hung up, Fiona typed the address into her computer. *Dr Curtis Morehead and his wife purchase restored Georgian Federal home, excellent example of Revolutionary War architecture. Dr Morehead is a professor of History at Williams College and his wife, Dr Elizabeth Hemphill, teaches English.*

Was the teen hiding in her parents' house? Fiona had seen a confined space, attic or closet with louvered doors. When she was pregnant with Mark she dreamt about sailboats. Water pulsed like a heart, tossed the boat to and fro, her cotton nightgown transparent with the tide. Eamon's hand was on her belly and then it was shaking her because her waters had broken and what she envisioned as a tadpole would become sandy-haired Mark, now a tall and thoughtful man. She closed her eyes, frogs beginning to sing outside and some kind of shrill bird that sounded like a baby screeched. When she awakened, Eamon was gone and the phone was ringing.

'Hello'. Fiona rubbed her eyes and looked at the clock. 8:00.

'Tell me everything you know about Dr Morehead and Dr Hemphill'.

'Who is this?'

'Detective O'Reilly, Williamstown Police Department. I understand you called very early this morning with information about the missing girl, Jessica Hemphill-Morehead'.

'Yes. You might have heard about little Joe Mullen in Salt Isle, New Hampshire'.

'The boy found in Louisiana? Some anonymous psychic from New Hampshire gave police the address'.

'I don't know about psychic. I have dreams. Jessica is at that address'.

'Ms Crenshaw. Jessica *lives* at that address. This isn't exactly a break in the case'.

'She's there, detective. I can't tell if she's safe or even alive but she's there'.

'Ok, we'll have a look. I must say I feel a little ridiculous calling those poor parents and asking if I can search the house again'.

Just last week she was daydreaming about a man she dated at nineteen, and then he contacted her on Facebook. Coincidence? She sang in his band, *Ahab's Rebels* the summer she waitressed on Cape Cod. She was Mark's age then, certain of nothing and surprised by everything. When Vic gave her a ruby necklace that he said washed up with the tide, she imagined for a time that he had the ability to pluck jewels out of the air or sea. She planned to stay on with him but a scholarship offered her another path and she took it. Now she visited his Facebook page every morning just to see his wild grey curls and those dimples.

Did you finish school?

Yes. I'm a nurse. You?

Used to be a fisherman. Bought that house on the bay.

Fiona thought of the silver flash, primal smell of the Atlantic at low tide and Vic's windburned face.

On the way to work, she stopped at Inky's Café for a non-fat cappuccino and a bagel. Eamon called on his morning break to tell her he'd be working late again. Mrs Singh went into labour at 3 and he doubted she'd deliver before eight or nine, first baby and all. *Don't hold dinner.*

When she got home, the light indicated voicemail. A message from Detective O'Reilly with a number to call back *right away*.

Fiona changed out of her uniform and put on a robe. Then she punched in the number. He answered on the first ring.

'We found her hanging in the basement closet off the laundry room. It's a closet they only use for off-season clothes. No one thought to look there. Apparently she hitchhiked home, took a handful of her mother's valium while her parents were at work. Left a note. Something about the pressure of school, and a boy who didn't ask her to the dance. Terrible tragedy. But what I want to know is how you did this'.

'I don't know, detective. I really don't know'. Fiona scribbled on the pad on the counter.

She hung up the phone and put her head in her hands. Suicide. She thought of her father and then Mark with his sunny disposition, safe in Ithaca. Good thing she never had another child.

On Wednesday, the calls started. Stories ran about her in the *Williamstown Record*, the *Salt Isle Bee* and even the *Boston Globe*. She helped find a Golden Doodle stolen from a yard and taken to Portsmouth, New Hampshire, and then a sixteen-year-old boy who hitched a ride to New York City to become a rapper. Both alive.

'Tell them you don't know anything. We're entitled to some peace, for God's sake'. Eamon reheated his salmon in the microwave so that steam came off of it like a puff of winter breath. Piping hot. Fiona envisioned him casting the line to catch his own salmon but his face looked like Vic's, high cheekbones and a long aristocratic nose.

Later that night she discovered she had a Wikipedia page: *Fiona Crenshaw, b. 1974, American psychic and modern day St Anthony*. The prisoner-of-war lost in Vietnam resurfaced in Costa Rica forty-five years later but she never found the baby snatched from a grocery cart or the bride who got into a Buick and disappeared.

Vic asked her if she could really find the missing.

Sometimes. Except not everyone wants to be found.

Guess I was lucky. Remember Melville?

A pregnancy scare at nineteen but she lost it and they named their almost child Melville. *He deserves a name*, Vic had said but it went beyond that as he invented a life for the hapless Melville, gave him an obsession with guitar picks and animal crackers.

You left your pick on the table again. Melville might choke.

Melville is smarter than that.

Fiona kept her iPad by the bedside table so she could look at Vic's face before she arose and started her day. Some mornings people queued, the line winding around the block, past Joey Mullen's house, decrepit men with walkers, and children holding onto adults' hands. There were parents who gave up children for adoption, divorced men and women seeking reconciliation with a spouse who had long ago moved on, and endless photos of Rambo and Fluffy.

Emilio wasn't the type to leave me. You have to do something, Miss. I pray to St Anthony every day, took out an ad in the paper.

Abby was too young to keep the baby but she's dead now and I just want a chance to know my granddaughter. See, here's her baby picture – just a few hours old. She'd be thirty-two now.

The urge to help moved through her, and her brain swirled with images of a swaddled infant, dark-haired man in an army uniform, and then her father hiding candy or pennies in his pocket before the indelible memory of the hole in his head intruded. Sometimes husbands and wives rang to tell her she was a charlatan, an instrument of the devil. Last week, a stone pitched through the porch window just missed her. Turned out that Emilio didn't

GROWING A NEW TAIL

So here we are, ten years after the honeymoon, and him clomping across the Florida café in his steel-toed boots to find a seat near the front window, cluttered with taped-on flyers advertising church bazaars and yoga lessons. Outside a few zinnias flap their limp petals in the humid puff of air they call a breeze around here. He pushes over a stack of *Time* magazines and newspapers to make room for his macchiato, double order of bacon, and sketchpad.

I sit on a cast iron chair near the back by the espresso machine. On the wall there's a painting of a woman in a gauzy dress kissing a man under a red umbrella, even though I swear it doesn't look like a speck of rain is falling, her dress all billowy and the blue-white of those tiny flowers that dot fields back home in the northeast. Kind of how it is with us; we prepare for rain where there isn't any, a damn hurricane or one of those funnel clouds that the airbrushed woman on TV with her tits hanging out of her v-neck gives a thirty percent chance of hitting somewhere, tearing up roads and picking up pets and even cars. Sometimes ten years can make a woman feel like life has caught her in a headlock, and she's choking on the monotony.

I think about Tim, how I'm pretty sure he's the kind of guy who'd refuse to leave his house if they evacuated for a storm. He'd be standing there in a muscle shirt and shorts, ready to tough it out. Oh, he'd tape up the windows and maybe have sandbags just in case. He'd also have a 12-pack of Sam Adams and movies loaded on the iPad.

Clem's the quiet kind. He eats too much and smokes those Maduro cigars so I'll probably be a widow someday, though God's a fickle sort, taking my Auntie Viv at forty-two and letting my bastard Grampy Murray live long enough to gamble away the family money. I order up an egg over easy and decaf, pretend not to see Clem's extra bacon though Dr Song warned him in April about saturated fat. Clem doesn't believe in anything but fate. *If it's my time, it's my time.* Fine. I'd like a guarantee that his time won't drag on for years, using up all our money.

'Anna, you're gonna marry me. You'll see'.

And I did, in a recycled ivory dress from the Goodwill, deli platters from Shop 'n Save. Our cake was donated by someone's sister-in-law, the flowers came from a funeral of a friend's grandmother, and Ricky and the Wildcats played their eighties disco music, since Ricky was my friend Sara's boyfriend. The whole wedding came in under three hundred dollars and that included the tux rental.

Beginnings don't matter, Clem said. We stayed in a Motel Six off the turnpike with a neon sign that blinked *V-CAN-Y*. No cable and a bed that sagged in the middle. I pulled up the edge of the bottom sheet to look for bedbugs, saw the yellowing mattress cover. Some honeymoon. None of this made a difference to Clem. We defined ourselves by what we lacked. No house, no kids, no pets. Nothing to lose.

'We're free, Anna. We could move to Florida, New Jersey, California'.

But we didn't move, stayed in a three room apartment until I finished the Licensed Practical Nurse programme, then we rented a two bedroom bungalow in the east side of town. Clem worked, I worked. We hated our jobs and spent everything we made on meals out so we didn't have to look at the rose and ivy wallpaper peeling away from the edges in the kitchen or the greyish-yellow tinge of the ceilings from all that cigar smoke. Until now, we hadn't even taken a vacation unless you count that weekend in Atlantic City. I bet Tim travelled, maybe on a safari in Kenya or to Paris to see the Eiffel Tower.

I could hear Clem crunching his bacon from across the room. I fingered the car keys in my pocket. Tim had told me to just walk out. *I'm excited thinking about it*, he said. He would meet me at the Dunkin Donuts in Port Orange to start our new life together. His grandmother had left him a sweet house in Daytona Beach, and he planned to sell surfboards and I'd get a job, maybe in a little café like this one, people in shorts and tropical prints having coffee, reading newspapers. I could learn to make drinks like cappuccinos and mochas, would greet the regulars by name, and have their drinks ready when they walked in the door. *Warm all year round.* I'd wear brightly-coloured sundresses and sandals. We'd have to spray for the mosquitoes though. I get welts from those suckers. Tim says the lizards are like the mice up north, wriggling in your house through the smallest gap. I wonder if they can grow new tails like salamanders. Once my cat caught one and it escaped, leaving just the tail in Blinky's surprised mouth. In a couple of weeks, that salamander would grow a new tail. We used to overturn rocks to find them, some with the stub of a new tail starting, like the nub of a finger I saw on the ultrasound before I miscarried.

My phone chirps but I ignore it, think of my backpack in our car, just earrings, shorts, jeans, and make-up I bought but never wore, though I'm thinking I'll start soon; coral lipstick, iridescent eye shadow and maybe some black eyeliner.

I'm going to have gold highlights streaked through my hair and wear those strappy-heeled sandals I saw in *Elle* magazine. I can see from the caller ID that it's Tim.

Then Clem catches my eye and winks. I take my sweet time walking over to his table, sashaying my hips and tossing back my brown curls like the Victoria's Secret models do on TV when they saunter down the catwalk in their silky underwear.

'Excuse me, mister. You look familiar', I say in my huskiest voice.

'Why don't you join me? What are you drinking?' Clem smiles, and I notice his green muscle shirt, white teeth and smooth skin with just a trace of shadow on his left check where the razor missed a patch this morning.

'Name is Maribelle', I say, offering my manicured hand.

Clem takes my hand in both of his big ones.

'I'm Timothy but you can call me Tim. Delighted to meet you, little lady'.

He shoves over the pad and bacon strips on a plastic plate.

I nibble on a slice of his bacon, tell him I'd like a double espresso over ice. No kids, no pets, no house. Maribelle and Tim. We can go anywhere.

MOSAIC

I strap my feet into the wobbly skates, pull up my yellow and black socks. On the drive to the park, the car in front of me has a bumper sticker that says 'Right to Bear Arms'. I need arms for counter balance when I skate. In the summer I reveal pale arms in my favourite lace-edged camisole. I've been lifting weights, going for definition. It's hard to live without arms but I can sure imagine a world without guns.

In college, I used to vomit up my breakfast, usually some sort of greasy moulded potato and the kind of scrambled eggs that had been sitting in a warming pan for hours. My mother had run off with a guidance counsellor from the middle school and my father would call me every night, after he'd had a whiskey or two.

'Hil'ry. What'm gonna do?'

'Take a class. Go to one of those meet-ups at the church', I'd say while I skimmed an Ibsen play or outlined my paper on Borges.

'Nah. Losers. What'm gonna do?'

Sometimes I composed a title for a country song, *Whiskey Heartbreak Blues*. I was twenty. What the fuck did I know about relationships? At that point in my life my focus was sticking my finger down my throat so I wouldn't get a pudgy roll around my middle. I also went on pointless dates with men too young to be interesting.

Roller blading is a dying art but I've always been about ten years behind the trends. I didn't get a smartphone until last year, would sit in the coffee shop tapping out texts by pressing the number until it got to the desired letter. It took five minutes to say *See you in an hour*. Mostly I just said *ok*. No one but Kent texted me anyway.

'You're like a seventies girl or something. Hippie chick'.

He looked like he'd sprinkled too much cocoa on his cappuccino and neglected to dab at his upper lip but it was actually a failed attempt to grow a moustache. Our list of compatibilities included yellow curry, cats, Ibsen and the colour pink. I'd long ago replaced bulimia with weight lifting and teaching. Leave the eating disorders to the young. Kent was the kind of skinny that required no maintenance so he sniped at the heroin chic models on TV. *Give the lady a transfusion*. He would have hated me ten years ago.

At thirty, I'm retro, sunburst tie-dye, two different coloured sneakers, rings on every finger and dreadlocks. I'm fashion challenged so I mix it up to make it seem intentional. No one at the university cares what I wear. I'm not on any administrative track, just made it to full-time last year.

Kent is gliding down the asphalt as if his feet had permanent wheels.

'Hey, Hill. Race you to the lake'.

I attempt a long stride, which is impossible in roller skates. My hot pink kneepads protect me as I hit the ground, straighten up, and inch forward in a move that is quasi-graceful. It's Saturday. After forty-five minutes of loops around the lake, we'll go to the Paper Crane Coffee Shop for espresso and then to my apartment for Saturday sex. He'll work on his dissertation and I'll polish some poems to send to the better journals. We'll eat something foreign, curry or Pad Thai.

When the earthquake hits, I'm perfectly balanced, at the end of our last run down the slight incline by the lake. Kent catches me when I fall and we hold each other with a kind of urgency that feels both familiar and unfamiliar. I once had a dream about being held tight enough to blur the lines between where my body ended and his began. The ground shakes and sputters while all around us people scream and run haphazardly. We know to drop to the ground, kneel there as if in prayer. Finally the shaking stops and the landscape calms. We take off our roller skates; sit cross-legged in our socks, holding each other's hands. I am partially perched on Kent's lap and we have more parts touching than when we make love. Maybe panic is a kind of lovemaking, a connection that takes its power from the possibility of death. We check each other out, gingerly stand up. Because aftershocks are common, we move away from the boat launch and parked cars.

Did I remember to send poems to *Paris Review* and *Prairie Schooner*, my only chance at immortality? Kent's dissertation is mostly done, portions of his work on Roethke already published.

I think about my father now living in a rent-controlled apartment in Rhode Island, far from earthquakes. We talk on the phone on Sundays. He doesn't drink anymore but he still calls me Hil'ry. *The world is going to shit*, he told me last week. *Terrorists wanna take over. You still writing po'try?* They let him have a small dog, a Maltese he calls Rudy. Sometimes I can hear a woman talking in the background.

There's a blot of yellow in the morning sky. We skirt around the rubble of branches, broken glass and throngs of people holding onto each other. A frizzy-haired woman is flanked by two hunky men, her glasses askance, their tattooed arms around her shoulders. Suddenly I have a craving for eggs Florentine. I can see myself sautéing the spinach, adding minced garlic. I think I'll die if I don't taste that combination again. When Kent grabs me, I'm imagining the tang of oily spinach on my tongue. We are almost at the intersection with its shattered walk light when we sink into a fissure that opens up in the middle of the sidewalk, my hand on his shoulder, his hand around my waist, a mosaic of green and red splinters and chunks of cement jabbing at our stocking feet.

HOUSE THE COLOUR OF DUSK

They had been told that their parents were killed in a break-in but Sienna knew better. A masculine-looking woman in a pinstriped suit, Mrs McDonald, showed up the next morning, told them they would have to leave town, use new names, Althea for Sienna, Leila for Nina. *Try to forget.* She said she understood that this wouldn't be easy but she also said, and this was the part that both of them remembered, that their lives might depend upon forgetting.

During a long ride in a station wagon, they learned about their new parents, Mr and Mrs Matthews. Mr Matthews was a Certified Public Accountant and Mrs Matthews taught Kindergarten. They had just moved from Tennessee because Mr Matthews had been transferred. Mrs McDonald pulled into the driveway of a red colonial in the kind of neighbourhood where children rode bicycles until dark and families had barbeques on summer nights.

'From now on, you are Althea and Leila Matthews. Your parents were transferred here. That's all you have to say. You'll have a week to adjust and then you'll start school'.

'We have your room ready. You like green and blue, right?' Mrs Matthews stretched her pink lipsticked lips into a smile.

Althea thought they weren't really married. She suspected that the entire world upon which her life had been built until this point was completely fake. She wasn't even sure her real parents had been her real parents though she recalled how people had said she looked like her mother. Leila resembled her father, a pensive looking man with a square jawline and a long torso.

In the beginning Althea thought she might wake up to find it had been a bad dream. A common occurrence for trauma survivors, Mrs McDonald had told them. *Post Traumatic Stress Disorder*, she called it, said they might benefit from medication, but Mrs Matthews talked her out of it. *They're children. We'll help them. It takes time.* Still Althea wondered if medication would have helped to mute the memories. The moans were worse than the screams because her parents were dying, in pain, and she didn't do anything to help them. If she had been older, maybe she would have broken the window right away, gone to Mr Stein's house and called the police before it was too late. She would never understand why they froze, hugged each other with closed eyes, listening to their parents die.

Knuckles had hammered relentlessly against the newly-painted white door that night, interrupting Sienna's science homework. The doorbell had broken ages ago and though their father had intended to replace it, it stayed on a *TO DO* list taped to the side of the refrigerator next to a cartoon of a couple reading that said, *We don't drink, we read. Can we offer you a book?*

Three men forced their way into the house, pushed Sienna and her little sister Nina roughly forward, telling Sienna to get in front and *shut it*. Then they opened the door to the basement. *Get down there and don't make a sound.*

Something heavy like the hutch was pushed against the door. Crouched next to the furnace in the dank-smelling darkness, they heard muffled conversation, their mother's high-pitched voice, their father shouting, glass smashing, something being dragged, then the guttural animal noises people make when they're in pain. By the time the front door slammed and a car revved, taking off into the brisk October night, Sienna and Nina were holding each other tight enough to cut off circulation. They stayed down there in the dark for what seemed like hours. Finally Sienna pulled the chain on the light bulb by the washing machine, broke the little window with a broom handle, and they helped each other outside into a perfect star-filled night, full harvest moon.

It was the kind of night their mother had loved. She would point out The Pleiades or Seven Sisters, Pegasus, the winged horse, and Cassiopeia, the Queen. They held hands and ran the half mile to Mr Stein's house, pounded with small hands on his door, tears streaming. When the police arrived, Nina had collapsed from terror and exhaustion.

At first they had nightmares. Mrs Matthews would sit with them, stroking their hair or bringing a mug of warm milk.

'I'm here. Not going anywhere. Do you want me to put on some music?'

Mozart sonatas reminded Leila of Sunday mornings with the classics on National Public Radio. Their father would have it on in the background while he whipped up pancakes or waffles.

Mrs Matthews baked elaborate pies and cakes. She lacked the acerbic wit of their mother and she had never read The Chronicles of Narnia or Mary Oliver's poetry. Mr Matthews liked Sudoku and he taught them how to figure out the number sequences. He would sit in a leather lounger after dinner and they'd hang over it, helping him.

Their father had liked to build a fire in the fireplace in winter, drink spiced cider in the evening, and have a family Scrabble game with popcorn on Saturday nights. Althea could remember her hand-embroidered Christmas stocking made by Grandma Tillie, aunts and cousins, all gone.

At first they practiced their names over and over. Althea liked the exotic sound of hers but Leila thought her new name was difficult to pronounce. Some people called her Lee-lah and others called her Lay-la or Lei-la. She preferred Lee-lah and since the name didn't come with a pronunciation that was what she told a parade of teachers, coaches, and social workers. Most of the kids in Kingsborough had lived in town all their lives and had grandparents who showed up at their choral concerts or to cheer for them at basketball games. Althea and Leila went home directly after school for the rest of the year. By the second year, Althea joined science club and Leila played softball on Wednesdays. Mr and Mrs Matthews never missed a game.

This might be our only chance, Althea told Leila, after the Matthews left for a two-day business trip to New York City.

'I'm scared. Can't we just stay home and order pizza? Ami and Tata left us money', said Leila.

'Well, I'm going. You can be a baby if you want to be'.

Hemmed in by rolling hills and farmland, the one road had been badly damaged in the blizzard of 2012, and the town never rebuilt, or at least no new road had shown up on Google maps.

'We need to look ordinary', Althea said.

Leila didn't know exactly what her sister meant but she chose a light grey dress, black tights, matching cardigan.

'Good walking shoes. It's at least a mile or so off of the main road'.

Between them, they had come up with sixty-seven dollars plus the pizza money. Heaving clouds were flanked by an almost turquoise sky. A slight hint of black fringed the edges, like the trail a plane leaves behind. In October, the trees were gaudy and in full array. Everything seemed infused with an otherworldly light.

'I'm hungry', Leila put her hand on her flat belly. It had been hours since they gulped down bowls of cereal and split a granola bar.

Only a Snickers bar and two packages of peanut butter crackers between them, they would have to hike back into town to buy dinner before the sun set.

Then the house was in front of them, directly at the bottom of the third hill. Rose-coloured, it stood like a sentry flanked by the gold and burgundy hillside. A shiver ran through Althea's body even as she felt sweat drenching her clothes. She pulled her thin sweater closer. Leila seemed frozen. Only ten on that long ago night, the memories unfolded in her mind like scenes in a movie. The first one had her sitting at their oak trestle table doing her reading homework while her mother told Sienna to finish the science questions and turn down her music. Her father sat in front of the computer. They never talked about his job but they were supposed to tell their friends that he was a computer programmer who worked from home for an internet company. If they asked. Most of the time no one cared what parents did for a living. It was only a teacher or two that inquired, especially around Career Day.

What does your father do for a living?

Uh, he works with computers. A programmer.

Do you think he'd be willing to come in and talk to our class about what programmers do?

Um, he's really busy. I'll ask.

Of course, he never went in and neither did her mother. 'We didn't even try to go upstairs. Do you think we should have? Maybe we could have saved them', Leila said.

'No. They would have killed us too. Mrs McDonald said that's why we had to have new names. We're the only ones who know what happened'.

'We don't really know though. Was Dad a spy?'

'I think he worked for the CIA. Remember when he was gone for a month?'

'How come we didn't have to go to court?'

'After Mrs McDonald came, she said they had everything they needed. They didn't want to put us through it. Justice will be served, she said. I wonder if they ever got the guys'.

Althea looked at the house again. She remembered the summer they decided to paint it a greyish-pink, *like dusk*, her mother had said. Her mother loved the sunsets in Medford. They all worked on painting, her father in faded jeans and a stained t-shirt that had a picture of Jim Morrison on it, her mother wearing khaki shorts with little paint stains on them. Later that night, they built a fire in the fire pit, toasted marshmallows and made s'mores and sang *Goodnight Irene* and a medley of Beatles' songs. It was past midnight when they went inside. Two months before the end of the life she knew. On Sunday morning her father made waffles. They drenched them in real maple syrup that filled the little hollows with amber sweetness. Then they sprawled out to read the *Sunday Times*. Nina got the comics, Sienna liked the fashion section and their parents read the rest of the paper.

'Do you want to go down the hill?' Leila looked at her big sister.

'I guess we should but I'm scared', Althea's teeth chattered.

'Me, too', Leila took Althea's hand and they walked through tickling yellow and green grass to their house the colour of icing and new scars.

They could see shades on the upper bedrooms, the light fixture on the farmer's porch. No furniture. Althea wondered what happened to everything. Her clothes had arrived in a large box, along with stuffed animals, a pillow, her bedspread. Both of them opened their boxes as if they expected a note from their mother and father. When they found only laundered and folded clothes, they closed them up again, stuck the boxes into the far reaches of their closet. Mrs Matthews took them shopping, and they picked out new clothes, sheets, pillows, and bedspreads. The only thing taken from those boxes was Leila's stuffed monkey, Raisin. She slept with it every night for the first two years. Now it was perched on her white dresser in the room they shared, even though the Matthews' house had four bedrooms.

'Don't you want your own room?' Althea's friend Brittany asked her.

'It's ok. Leila is fine'.

'God, I'd never want to share a room with Lauren. She's so immature'.

Althea didn't think she could sleep alone. If she awakened in the night, Leila would crawl into bed with her and she'd do the same when Leila woke up whimpering. They'd hold each other close, squeeze their eyes shut and wait for morning.

The front door was locked. Althea went around to the back door. Also locked. There was a sign on the back door that said *No Trespassing*. The basement windows were new with yellow manufacturer's stickers still on them. In the kitchen, the toaster was gone, the blender, her mother's set of cobalt blue mugs on the mug rack, all gone. Two chairs stood in the middle of an unfamiliar black and white linoleum floor. Althea had a bitter taste in her mouth. The living room. It happened in the living room. The thump of chairs, the initial gasp and shrieks from her mother.

'No, no. Oh, my God. Please. The children'.

Shoes stomped on the wooden floor, and finally there were the moans that would follow her for the rest of her life. *Your parents were very brave*, Mrs McDonald had told them. When Althea asked how, she didn't answer.

Althea took Leila's hand and they walked around to the front, four narrow farmhouse windows that her mother had loved. She had positioned the sofa facing the windows, told them they should always have furniture facing the light. *It might not be Feng Shui but I like it.* Beige fabric shades helped with the winter chill but most of the time they were pulled up, *to let in the light*. Althea crept closer. Two shades were mostly down but two were up. They were holding hands so tightly that Althea's fingers began to grow numb. Leila started to whimper, pushing back the wild hair blowing into her eyes. The wind had picked up and the dry grass stood up like quills.

A patch of sunlight gilded the oak floor. No upholstered chairs, blue sofa, or wicker rocking chair, the one her mother said she'd rock them in to soothe them when they were babies. An electric sander was propped next to the wall, and the floors looked refinished, shiny. The walls were pure white, fresh paint white. Althea had been scared there would be bloodstains but it was just a shell of a house where her family once fought about taking too long in the bathroom, how many chocolate chip cookies were too many, bedtimes and chores. A family that spent winter Sundays reading in front of the fire, interrupting each other to share passages.

Nina reached for Sienna.

See-see, she said.

Neenie, Sienna whispered back.

Arm in arm, they turned and high-stepped through prickly grass, beyond the climbing tree with its garnet dots of leaves, the house growing smaller.

STORM

I always thought I'd die a violent death, sure as I know I ain't living to see no grandchildren. Oh, it's not for lack of wishing, I'm always wishing. My momma used to say, *Della, you come down to earth now. You up there so high you gonna singe your eyebrows on the sun.* Used to be what I knew was just inconvenient – like knowing the potatoes ain't ready when we gotta harvest.

My John don't hold much stock in any of it. He's a practical man, though what I know about him I ain't gonna say. A married woman learns to keep her mouth shut.

'Della, it's fixing to storm. Let's get the tomatoes picked so they don't get bruises on em'.

And he was right. He smelled the electric wind I felt in my bones yesterday. Yet the sun was out and most people were going about their business, riding bicycles and chatting over fences 'bout that stupid war we ain't got no business fighting, and those school shootings. In Mercy, there's a whole lot of fence chatting. These days, it's mostly about poor Peggy and her problem. I ain't the gossiping type but Peggy's 'bout the homeliest girl in all these parts.

Her nose ain't put on right and she's got the kind of hair all the hair gel in the county ain't gonna cure. Even her eyes are mismatched, one bigger and rounder than the other. As if the good Lord didn't think that was enough, he made her bow-legged and all her weight settled from her waist down, giving her practically no melons at all, more like plum tomatoes. But she is nice as homemade ice cream on a July afternoon, always a smile and maybe some peach muffins. Her passion is gardening and she even drove herself all the way to the city for some certification class as a Master Gardener. When she turned up expecting, and just twenty without any prospects, none of us could figure it out. My John thought she was taken advantage of probably by some city guy, but who would be mean enough to do that to Peggy? Thing is, Peggy ain't talking. She just go about her business like it's a case of poison ivy or something, asking Mrs Curry for some medicine for the unsettled stomach and later for the hemorrhoids. Mrs Curry better than any doctor and she work for free. John says it's a darn shame about Peggy since her mother has the multiple sclerosis. Mary-Ann was a good-looking woman. Still is 'cept she can't walk for beans.

Tuesday and not a lick of work has been done. The air is like pipe smoke, all thick and heavy, hanging in dark clouds. Momma used to say this was tornado weather but we ain't had a twister since I been here.

'Hey there'.

Young man with a bolo tie and a perfectly-shaped cowboy hat.

'Hello'.

'I'm new around here. Got any work for a farmhand?'

'Nah. We only got this one horse, some fields', I waved my hand at the acre field and Willy, our old horse.

'What else do you do?'

Now I'm polite as the next person. My momma didn't bring me up to be rude but this man seemed a mite nosy. I wanted to give him a smartass answer like 'circus performer' or 'librarian' but I figured it might make him mad.

'We just make things, that's all'.

'What kind of things?'

Mr Clean Shoes and Sharp Hat was getting to me. We don't make no doilies, I can tell you that.

'Y'know. Just the things folks use – stools, chairs, boxes. Like that.

'Oh, you're cabinetmakers?'

The man not too smart, I could tell that right off. We don't make cabinets. Dalton Walberg makes the cabinets in town, everyone knows that. Woodworking is what we call it in these parts and my John is good at it. I'm not so bad either. My rocking chair is kinda famous for the new mothers. It's said that a Della chair will put any crying babe to sleep. But I didn't tell him all that.

'Isaac Jermaine', he stuck out a hand that was clean as a young girl's.

I wiped my hand on my jeans and shook it.

'Know anywhere where I could pick up some temporary work? Gas is expensive'. He thumbed toward his truck, a nice green Ford sitting by the side of the road.

I got to thinking about Peggy and how she might be able to use some help with her mother an invalid, and no daddy.

'There's the farm down the road, red silo. That's Mary-Ann's place. She's got the MS and her daughter is expectin'. They might be able to do with a spot of help'.

The man tipped his hat and headed toward the truck but not before he fixed me with this stare. I can't describe it. It was a combination of sadness and something else, best I could guess. I was glad when he got in that truck and drove away but then I got to wondering about Peggy and Mary-Ann and if I did right sending him over to a place with two defenceless women.

'Mary-Ann?' She picked up the phone on the first ring probably because she kinda sits right by it when walking is bad for her.

'Yeah?'

'Did some man in a fine hat come up to your place yet? He looking for work and I thought you might have some but there's something strange 'bout him. Can't put my finger on it. I just glad when he left. Sorry to tell you this but I thinking maybe I shouldn'a sent him over'.

'No man come here'. I could hear her chair scrape as she went to the picture window to look outside. 'Nope. No one 'cept Peggy in the garden'.

'How you doin'?'

'Can't complain or if I did no one would listen'. Mary-Ann laughed. 'Storm's comin'. Peggy thinks it's gonna be a bad one. She says she senses things 'cause of her condition and all'.

'Does seem kinda dark. I'd better put the storm windows down and feed Willy. You be careful now. Call if you need anything, 'kay?'

Then I saw the truck again, pulling around the bend after Bailey's Creek. Going way too fast, if you ask me. Pretty soon he's stepping on the brakes and I can hear them squealing. Damned if he don't tip his hat to me then go right past like he's in a real hurry. That's when I heard the phone.

'Hello'.

'Della – it's Mary-Ann. You didn't see Peggy, did you? She was tending the garden like she always do and I called her in for lunch. She don't answer and I been yellin' and yellin'. Thought maybe she dropped by your place to help you get ready for the storm'.

'Nope. Nobody here but that man I told you 'bout. He just drove by here again, tipped his hat. I could get John to go looking for Peggy'.

'That would be neighbourly of you, 'preciate it. Getting kinda nervous with the storm coming and all and Peggy close to her time'.

I could hear John tinkering with the back window. When I told him about Peggy, he put out our sandwiches so we could eat before he went looking. My John makes a good cold meatloaf sandwich with plenty of ketchup, just the way I like it.

Gotta mend the fence out back by the barn for the third time. I don't mind it. John ain't no good at those things. He tends to the kitchen; I do the mowing and the gardens. He makes a peach pie that would make a man put down his gun. I ain't kidding. Way I look at it is I'm lucky. I don't have to sit in the hot kitchen making biscuits and pies; I get to be in the great outdoors, where God want me to be. My momma, bless her soul, frowned on it. *Ain't natural for a man to be doing woman's work,* she'd say. I don't know what's natural. Peggy pregnant ain't natural, but there she is shuffling around. Fighting wars ain't natural but Tommy Lescoe died last year in Afghanistan and he weren't no older than our girl Molly. She married Michael Redfern and moved to Atwoodville last year. We don't have no son to help around here, no daughter neither since Molly left. I miss the company. She'd help with the pickin' and the mowin' and all. In the winter, we'd sit by the fire and make sweaters for the ones in town who ain't got 'em.

Soon as we done eating I shoo John out so I can wash up and he can get to the business of finding Peggy. Storm clouds gettin' closer so I get my tools and head to my fence mending. Then I see him again. He's driving slower this time, coming round the bend at the creek as if he meaning to stop, and I swear there's someone beside him, maybe a child because I can only see the top of a brown head down in the passenger seat. I want to ask him about Peggy but then he speed up, tipping his hat at me like before. I'm wishing I could call John but he ain't got no cell phone. We just got the cable in the county last year. I hear the phone again and run so fast I almost trip on the braided rug.

'Della? It's Mary-Ann again. Did you see that man you talked of in the Ford truck? Red McDuffy says he seen someone look like Peggy in that truck'.

'He just drove by, tipped his hat again. Want me to run down the road, see if I can spot him?'

'No. Red is here. He'll take the truck down; go looking round your place. If he come back, could you try to stop him?'

'Sure, Mary-Ann. Now don't you worry. I'm sure he a nice man'.

Mary-Ann's got more troubles than any folk deserve and I don't need to be addin' to them. Truth be told, I'm pretty worried myself. Whoever in that truck was either hiding or half-lying down. Peggy ain't no child-sized woman, especially now that she expecting and all. Between John and Red, they'd find him. Our county ain't big and there's only one main road out of here. I wish we got the cell phone like some folk have.

Getting late and I can't keep my mind on the fence mending though I manage to get Willy water and put him in the barn. I figure about an hour till the skies open up. No time to cut back the big tree next to the barn but that tree, she's weathered a lot of storms and probably this one as well. Then I see John coming up the road. I'm always glad to see him but now 'specially.

'What's the news?'

'I couldn't find the man but people say he took off out of town with poor Peggy in his truck. That man up to no good and she expectin' and only twenty'.

John look like he about to cry. We got a daughter and we always worry when she that age when young men come sniffing round but none of us thought Peggy would have that problem, being homely and all.

'You shoulda let me know when the man stopped. I might have been able to do something'.

I know he sayin' this because he feels guilty. I do, too. But truth be told, I handle the outside stuff; he handle the inside stuff. Been like that for twenty-four years. I never think to ask him to help anymore than he asks me to make sweet potato pie. Peggy, she like my own daughter – two years younger than Molly and they going to the same school and all. She helped with the birthing of piglets, stood up for Molly at her wedding. Molly offered to come and help with the baby after the birth. If anyone knows the father of Peggy's baby, it'd be Molly but she swear to me she don't know, that Peggy ain't talking even to her good friend.

That's when I think to call Molly. It's a distance call so we don't talk more than once a week on Sundays but this important.

Molly picks up on the second ring. When she hear my voice, she worried.

'You ok, Ma?'

'Fine. It's Peggy. She gone missing'.

Molly laughs. 'Peggy is in labour. She's at St Edward's Hospital. Some man just called me about ten minutes ago. I'm heading out there in a little bit. You want me to call you when we know if it's a boy or girl?'

I tell her about the man in the green Ford truck but she don't know who he is and I know we both thinking he somehow connected to our Peggy. I don't think it good for Peggy to be hanging with a strange man. I miss my Molly. She a good daughter. Never in trouble like Peggy and smart in school. She want to go to college and Mike swear he gonna get the money to send her so she can be a teacher.

John still worried. He wants to head out toward the hospital and I let him go. I'm gonna stay by the phone and wait for Molly to call. Then I see the truck. He's pulling into my drive and I'm wishing I hadn't let John go. The man gets outta the truck this time. I don't see no passenger. He knocks at my door.

'Ma'am. Just wanted you to know that I brought Peggy to the hospital. I found her in the field moaning. Her water broke and it seemed urgent. She told me her daddy lives here and I should let him know that he has a new grandson'.

'Peggy's daddy don't live here', I said, twisting my red kerchief and feeling uncomfortably hot all of the sudden.

'You Della?'

'Yep'.

Mr Jermaine wrinkles up his forehead so he look maybe forty for a minute.

'I'm sure she said Della's husband. John, right?'

'John my husband. He the daddy of Molly. Ain't no daddy to Peggy'.

He look deep in thought, runs those girl hands of his 'round the rim of that fine hat he was wearing.

'I'm sorry, Ma'am, but I'm quite sure she said John was her daddy. She told me this before, in the city'.

'Before?'

Mr Jermaine shuffles his good boots and looks down.

'I'm going to marry her. Going to ask her daddy's permission. I was raised to do the right thing'.

I held the door open so Mr Isaac Jermaine could come in because I need to sit down. I wasn't gonna set out no plates for cake and tea but I need to sit down and he may as well sit down with me.

'You the father?'

He nods.

'You telling me you is the father of Peggy's boy and Peggy is the daughter of my John?'

'I guess that's what I'm telling you. I'm sorry Miss Della. I thought you knew. I met Peggy at that Horticultural Show last fall. She knows a lot about plants, you know. She's going to be a Master Gardener'.

'Name is Mrs Watkins , I said

It ain't me that's gonna die the violent death, I think. It's you, John, Peggy, Mary-Ann, the whole lot of you. A clap of thunder so loud, I thought it hit the willow tree out back shakes the whole house, then sideways rain splatters the windows.

John comes bursting through the back door, tracking water all over the floor, shit-eating grin on his face.

'It's a boy. Peggy's gone and had a little boy. Della, ain't it grand, ain't it grand?'

Open and shut case is what Kevin said. He's my lawyer, married to my sister June. I didn't even spend the night in the holding cell. Good old Kevin arranged it all. He said not to worry but to wear something conservative for the hearing. I picked out a grey suit with a white button-down, shined my shoes with the little kit that came with the shoe polish. Rachel used to shine my shoes and iron my shirts. I never had a girlfriend who did that before. She *liked* taking care of me.

Why did they make our relationship sound criminal? *Stalking* instead of checking up on. That's all I did. Made sure she was ok. I love Rachel. Maybe a person only finds that kind of love once or twice in a lifetime. First time for me. She told me she loved me, did little things that backed it up. I figured I had some rights. Relationships are two-way, aren't they? I don't pretend to be any kind of expert on women but I think I know Rachel pretty well.

Kevin is kind of dorky looking but he's good to June. Their kids are better looking than both of them, which makes me think that maybe there's a genetic thing that happens when two unattractive people mate. It's like the best genetic material went into Sibyl and Les. I mean they're really cute. And smart. Les is only three but he knows all his numbers and letters, writes his name and a few other words. Sibyl is two. I thought I'd have a couple of kids when I marry Rachel. Maybe they wouldn't be plump like her because I'm skinny. She has nice eyes. They could get her eyes, my build. I even decided I'd propose on Valentine's Day. We'd go to Shasta over on Second Avenue. They have maroon tablecloths and real flowers in little vases. Rachel loves the sirloin there. This was just in the thinking stages. She had *oohed* and *ahhed* at rings whenever we passed jewellery stores so I kind of thought she was dropping me a hint. A lot had happened in our relationship since she rear-ended me a year ago.

When I get to the diner, Kevin is sitting there in the red-cushioned booth drinking black coffee. I slide in across from him. Everything about the place is cheery; the daisies on the plastic placemats, the little pies rotating in a lit glass case, our twenty-something server with red pigtails tied with yellow yarn. The world here is a fucking slice of cherry pie served on a blue glass plate.

'Hi Kevin'.

'Shawn'. He tips his head in the way men do when they don't want to shake hands. Hell, I wash my hands as much as the next guy.

'So, why did you do it?' He looks up at me, brown eyes with a beginning furrow between his bushy eyebrows.

'Do what? I told you. Out of concern for her. She started seeing this psycho date from that whacked-out website'.

'Shawn. You looked in her windows, parked in her driveway at three am and beeped your horn. And you threatened Ron'.

'He deserved it. He was going to hurt her. Only a matter of time. He's one of those sociopaths – make her trust him, then move in for the kill'.

'He's an insurance agent, Shawn. Lives with his mother. Mows his grandmother's lawn'.

'What kind of man in his thirties lives with his mother? That ought to tell you something'.

'You can't use that as a defence, Shawn. You want me to call his mother to the witness stand? Not a crime. Answer my question. Why'd you do it?'

'I told you. I love her. I was going to propose'.

'Ok. We'll go with the broken heart thing. Irrational. Jilted lover. But Ron is pressing charges for the email threat you sent him. Never send anything over the internet. You should know that. You work with computers'.

'What threat? My duty to help him understand Rachel'.

'If I'm going to work with you, you have to be honest with me. In what reality is *stay the fuck away from Rachel or else* not a threat? And what about the car? What on earth were you thinking?'

'A joke. I told you he's a psycho. No sense of humour. It was only a little piece of rope'.

'Made into a noose and hung from his rearview mirror. Not funny, Shawn. I don't think anyone would find that humorous, and the police have a photograph'.

'He's not even seeing her anymore. I told you he was bad news'.

'Don't you think it might be a little scary to go out with a woman who has a stalker ex-boyfriend?'

'You're my lawyer, Kevin. You're supposed to be on *my* side'.

'I am on your side. I just want you to know what we're up against. I need facts. Today is just a preliminary hearing in the judge's chambers'.

'You know how I know Rachel loves me?'

'Not listening, Shawn'.

'I know she loves me because we had good sex. She looked right at me. Ever have a woman look right at you when she's coming?'

'I can't believe we're even having this conversation. Rachel has made it very clear that she isn't interested. You've crossed a line and now you're going to court. Get a grip'.

'Yeah, well, you've been married a long time. I can't expect you to understand. This is a game she's playing. She wants to see how far I'll go to win her back. I know Rachel. No means yes'.

'No means no. At least in the eyes of the law'.

'Don't worry. I'll say what I need to say to get out of this. But I know the truth. You want to know what I used to call her? Little apricot because of her – you know. She called me Chorizo'.

'Damn it, Shawn. Let me do the talking'.

He wants facts; I'll give him facts. I'll send the email when I get home. He can lawyer it up so they'd understand.

To: *kevinlanchesteresq@conlonlaw.com*
From: *shawnthedude@telonet.net*
Subject: *You've Got My Back!*

My defence, Kevin: I love her. It's the kind of love that starts in your toes, moves all the way up your body. It started almost a year ago. She encouraged it. In fact, I'd say she revelled in it at first. Probably never before had that kind of attention from anyone. I don't know if you've met her but she doesn't exactly have movie star looks. She's a little on the plump side and her skin is kind of blotchy, especially certain times of the month.

At first she loved me back. I made her feel beautiful, she said. We'd stay up all night talking and well, making love. As I said, she's kind of hefty but I liked all those curves. So feminine. She had beautiful breasts, well-shaped with pink nipples. God, I loved to suck on those pink nipples. And she smelled great. I don't know what it is about smell but a woman either smells wrong or right. Sometimes we'd stay in bed all weekend, turn down the volume on our phones. Once my mother even drove over to the apartment because she couldn't reach me. It was January, kind of slushy outside. As you know, my mother doesn't walk so well and I'm in a second floor walk-up so it took her a long time, clomping up those stairs and us peeking out the window, laughing. I didn't want to explain Rachel to Mom. I called her later. You know I'm not a bad son, Kevin.

It was good with Rachel for a long time. Six months is a long time, isn't it? Before Rachel, my longest relationship was two months. Ellen Gordimer. She worked in the next cubicle and someone fixed us up. We were fixer uppers. I'd wait for her outside her therapist's office and then we'd go for Italian and she'd cry into the antipasto. No one had ever loved her, not even me, though I tried. She got on my nerves with her habit of thrusting out her bottom lip and mispronouncing words. I told her I was seeing someone else which wasn't even true. I was reading this book about positive thinking and I thought I could manifest a better relationship if I said it out loud. I wanted to be seeing someone else. Then Rachel rear-ended me at a stoplight.

Totally my fault is what Rachel said, and it was. I was obeying the traffic laws but she was drinking from her travel cup and checking her phone calendar. Doing more than one thing at a time has never worked for Rachel. She'd tell you that herself. It didn't cause much damage but we had to call the police and stand there for hours in the March wind making phone calls and filling out forms. By then we knew each other pretty well. I asked her out.

She said yes, Kevin. You can put that on the court record. She loved me or at least that's what she said over and over. Not at first, of course. We did the obligatory things couples do when they're getting to know each other. I even took her home to meet Mom though you know Mom doesn't like anyone her children date. Rachel did ok though, complimented her cooking and even cooed over her collection of cat figurines even though I know she hates that kind of stuff. Mom was worried about Rachel's weight, said she would blow up like a whale if we ever had kids.

It was a Thursday when she told me. Met someone else. Goddamn Internet dating site. soulmates4ever.com. She's not that pretty; you've seen that for yourself. She's the girl next door except she's my girl next door, not Ron Lyon's. I didn't even know she used a computer for anything but email. You think you know someone.

I guess I had noticed her backing off in September. I sent flowers, not roses but close. I had asked my mother what she thought and she said

Rachel probably wanted a commitment. For women of a certain age, this is important. That's when I started planning our engagement. I'm not rich but I do ok. We could be comfortable, maybe buy a townhouse or a raised ranch. I tried steering Rachel to jewellery stores again but this time she didn't seem interested. Maybe I waited too long.

Do your best, Kevin. And give Sibyl and Les a hug from their Uncle Shawn.

On Thursday, I report to the courthouse. I'm ushered into a big room with a conference table and upholstered chairs – the judge's chambers. Kevin motions to a seat next to him and I wait for Rachel to come through the double-panelled door. I'd even worn a dab of her favourite cologne.

'Doesn't Rachel have to be here?' I whisper to Kevin, straightening my tie knot. I could never tie these things. That was Rachel's job.

'No. She's represented by counsel', he says but he's speaking through his teeth. 'Don't say anything. Not a word'.

After papers are slid across the table, Kevin begins his spiel.

'Your Honour, my client was overcome with grief at the loss of the relationship. He's assured me that he's sorry for what he did'.

Sorry I didn't hurt the guy for stealing away my Rachel. We had plans; marriage and kids kind of plans. It's not her fault that she's dumb about the internet. What about my email? Did Kevin even read it? I stare at a scratch on the table, fingernail or penknife. Once I carved our initials on a tree in the park, tried to make a heart but it looked more like boobs.

Ron's lawyer hems and haws about stupid stuff like where the car was parked and whether or not I have a driver's license. He wants to know if I broke into the car (it was open) and how I knew it was Ron's car. These guys go to college a long time to learn this? A skinny woman in a pantsuit with spiky hair was representing Rachel. What did she know about this stuff? Kevin says the case will be continued but he's hopeful that we'll settle out of court, no trial or anything. I'll have to pay a fine and Kevin says there will definitely be a restraining order preventing me from contacting Rachel. Unless she contacts me, which I'm pretty sure she'll do now that Ron is out of the picture.

Rachel, I'll wait for you for as long as it takes. Just give me a sign. I won't tell anyone about our game. Hell, I will even go to jail for you if that's what you want. I bought the engagement ring today. It's resting on top of the night table in its little velvet cage. Remember the ring you looked at all those months ago in the window of Winslow and Davit? Blood drop rubies and a sprinkling of diamond chips? That's the one. I took out a loan, baby. Game over. Claim your prize, apricot.

ASYMMETRY

Madame Indigo's specialty was communicating with recently departed loved ones, testimonials on a laminated sheet were taped to the side glass:

> Now I can sleep at night, knowing that Ethan is in a better place. Madame Indigo is a Godsend.
>
> Nigel spoke to her and I know he's at peace. Madame Indigo has a calling.

The *Psychic Journeys* sign said it would open at eleven o'clock but the violet door was bolted and a rose-coloured shutter dotted with stars blocked the window. Philomena shivered in her threadbare coat, fingered the folded over envelope in her inside pocket, seventy-four dollars, saved from the last three month's social security checks. She was going to use it to pay part of the oil bill and then go to Ed's Diner. It had been days since she had a proper meal, and she had been looking forward to the lunch for a week. She didn't know what Madame Indigo charged but she hoped no more than fifty. The oil company could wait.

She used to go to Ed's Diner with Alan, order up a basket of fish or sometimes fried shrimp and chips sopping up grease on the blue and white paper. Alan would douse the whole thing in ketchup so that it looked like a bloody accident. *Ah, Phily. If that's the only thing you've got to complain about, you ain't got no worries. No worries a 'tall.*

At breakfast every day she missed watching him look at the birds at the feeder and the crinkle of his smile when he saw a black-capped chickadee, his favourite. *Pretty bird. No squirrel will raid the feeder while I'm here.* Philomena didn't know the names of any other birds, forgot to restock the feeder with sunflower seeds, hang the suet in October. No one paid attention to the brush and leaves strewn across the lawn, but it wasn't any better when Alan was alive. He had never liked yard work in spite of her nagging. Eventually Mrs Prendergast sent over her son, Christophe to do it. Philomena would bake a pie and have Alan bring it over, just to get him out of the house for a few minutes.

When Alan died on a rainy Sunday, his illness had already cost a fortune. Some of it was covered by insurance, but the rest remained like a stain on her credit. Now the yellow collector's letters accumulated like daily banners in her mailbox. *Overdue. Important. Open immediately.*

Don't you worry, Phily. We won't be buying a holiday home on Cape Cod but we've got enough. Just me and my Phily growing old together. They never discussed dying, though he worried about the baby birds on cold spring days. *I hope they make it, Phily. Their wee bodies aren't made for this kind of cold.* After paying credit card bills, final expenses and car repairs, the savings account dwindled to six hundred dollars. Their daughter, Maeve, paid for the funeral luncheon at The Hillside. Just a few neighbours and friends, Maeve and Bobby and their son, little Rob. Everyone called him *Little Rob* so as not to mix him up with Bobby, as if a six-year old might be mistaken for a thirty-seven-year-old man. Little Rob had called Alan,

Papi. *Where did Papi go?* He asked. Maeve pointed to the ceiling.

'Papi's in heaven, little Rob. He's looking down at you right now, sweet cakes'.

Maeve arranged everything; the plain mahogany box with twisted brass handles, a CD of Willie Nelson singing *Amazing Grace*, snapdragons and iris on the altar and a simple eulogy delivered by Fr Merrill. Philomena was, for once, speechless. How dare he die, leaving her to manage everything alone? What happened to growing old together?

Philomena wanted to know where Alan went after death. If he knew about any other sources of money, that would be extra – *icing on the cake*, Alan would have called it. Maeve tried to send her a little something each month but Philomena saved it. Some days she would eat only one meal and a snack. Lentils, an onion, and carrots made her a soup that lasted all week. Her mouth was watering for pot roast, salad, potatoes, and a slice of almond cake with real buttercream frosting. Maeve had her job at the bank but she had her own family to worry about. Bobby's landscape work was seasonal and the snowless winter wasn't helping his plowing business. Little Rob had an overbite and would need braces someday. Still she was glad she had a daughter nearby. Maeve was the one who made her get dressed, go back to her crocheting and weekly trips to the library for a romance novel or mystery, though lately she found herself looking at the same page over and over, the words jumping around like little bugs. Maybe she needed new glasses or a different kind of book.

A large woman in a long forest-green dress and matching cape waddled toward the door. Her oversized felt hat had a curiously placed blue glass jewel on one side as if she had mistakenly pinned it there instead of in the middle where it belonged. Philomena wanted to reach out and straighten it, like she used to do when Maeve was learning to button and missed buttons or buttoned her shirt wrong.

Do it myself, Maeve would insist. Philomena would right the buttons before she went off to preschool. She didn't want anyone to think she was neglectful like her own mother. Pouring her cereal at six, walking to the bus stop alone while her mother slept it off. No, Maeve would have tidy braids, a properly buttoned outfit, and a neat lunch packed in her pink plastic lunch bag. There would be carrot sticks, an apple, and a sandwich on whole grain bread. Milk to drink. No soda.

'Can I help you?' Madame Indigo produced a single key hanging on a keychain with a dangling crystal ball.

'Um. I'd like a reading, if possible. I mean I want to contact my husband. He's passed'. Philomena looked up at the sky.

'I know', Madame Indigo sighed. 'Very sudden, it was'.

'What do you charge?' Philomena pulled her worn-out coat closer. Maeve said she would order her mother another coat online. Something warm for the long Connecticut winter.

'That coat is too old, Mother. The lining is frayed and there's a rip by the shoulder'.

'I can sew that. No need to spend the money'.

'Mother, you need it. I'm going to send you one from Penney's when I get paid. A nice wool coat. Camelhair, with a belt'.

A month had gone by but Philomena knew that Maeve had been promoted to head teller at the bank and also taught catechism. The brakes on the van had gone and they had to fix the roof. The coat could wait. If she wore two sweaters underneath, she almost didn't notice the biting wind. Alan would have said that it was impractical to buy a coat when the old one could be repaired. Fashion and warmth were beside the point to him. His L.L. Bean wool sweater had holes that she had darned over and over.

Madame Indigo studied her for a moment then held the door open. Red velvet curtains covered the back window and some kind of sparkly material was draped over the walls. In the centre of the room a plum-coloured chair was pulled up to a table with painted-on stars. A flat piece of glass about a half-inch thick set in a leather case rested on the table next to what looked like Tarot cards.

'Fifty dollars. Ok, forty. No credit cards though. Madame Indigo won't operate on credit'. Madame Indigo removed her purple leather gloves.

Philomena felt her body relax. She'd have enough for lunch and maybe that piece of pie.

'Yes. Yes, I want a reading. What do you need to know?'

'Name of your departed'.

Madame Indigo motioned to a ladder-back chair, told Philomena to put her bag on the table.

'Alan. Alan Montague'.

'Date of death'.

'20 October. Three months ago. I'm Philomena. Philomena Montague. Alan called me Phily'.

'Madame Indigo knows who you are'.

Then Philomena noticed Madame Indigo's feet, red leather shoes with little flower and leaf etchings on them. Pointy toes. Fairy shoes, she thought. There was a time Maeve wanted sneakers covered with brightly-coloured butterflies and a little light that flickered when she moved, flashing brighter when she ran. *Magic sneakers,* she called them. Philomena couldn't convince her that it was a marketing ploy, adding glitter and lights to ordinary sneakers that Maeve would outgrow in six months. *Ah, get 'em for the girl. She doesn't ask for much, y'know,* Alan had said. It was true. Maeve never wanted the American Girl dolls or video games so popular with her peers. A birthday gift and worth it to see her whole face open in a wide smile.

'Magic sneakers!' She wore them every day until the butterflies faded to colourless moths and her toes poked out the end. Then she kept them by her bedside after Philomena replaced them with gold-laced purple sneakers. Even then, she'd catch Maeve looking wistfully at the worn-out sneakers banished to her closet.

Madame Indigo sat down, put her forefinger on her forehead as if she was deep in thought.

'Close your eyes'.

A strange music began to play, kind of harp-like with a bristly percussion in the background. She heard rustling and then a thump.

'Spirit. Come. Oh, spirit of the departed Alan Montague. Give us a sign'.

Another thump and then a scrape as if a chair had been pushed back.

'Your Phily is here. She wants to know if you're ok. What's that? Should I tell her?'

'What? What did he say?' Philomena could feel a chill even though the room was warm when she walked in. A cold wind seemed to be hovering right over her chair. Then there was a tinkling noise like a faint bell or chime.

'He's worried about you. Says he's sorry he didn't save more'.

'Is he in Heaven?'

'Yes'.

'Ask him what it's like'.

'It's like floating, he says. Like the time you were on that boat somewhere warm'.

'Florida. We went on a cruise years ago'. Philomena remembered sitting on the chaise lounge, listening to the ocean lapping. It seemed as if all the air had been swallowed by the sea, leaving just a wave of heat, like the moment when she opened the oven to take out a pie.

More music and another couple of thumps.

'Can you ask him about insurance? We never talked about money'.

Philomena opened one eye to see Madame Indigo's face screwed up as if trying to solve a problem. Madame Indigo looked at the glass rectangle on the table, and then touched a cameo brooch on her chest. Perched on the edge of her seat, it looked as if she might tumble off any moment.

'Does the letter *T* mean anything to you?'

Some mail a while back had a large T on the envelope but Maeve had told her to be careful about opening junk mail. *They're usually looking for money, Mother.* She'd have to remember where she put it. It was probably in the basket or stuffed into her purse.

She wanted to ask if Alan still had white stubble on his chin and a bald spot on the back of his head. Did death preserve how you looked when you died or were you restored to your youthful self? Alan had been rugged and handsome in his twenties and thirties before he started balding and putting on weight.

'He misses you and someone else. A child? Does the number three mean anything to you?'

Philomena screwed up her forehead. Three. Little Robbie started first grade on September third.

'I'll bet it's little Robbie. He started school on the third. Little Rob called him Papi. In the summertime, they'd play checkers and catch. Little Rob is getting big. Tell Alan he'd be proud of him'.

'Yes. It's little Robbie he's talking about. He's glad little Robbie is doing well'.

When the hour was up, Philomena noticed the sun had come out and even though it was January, it seemed bearable. She walked across the street to Ed's diner, ordered up her fish and chips. She had given two twenties to Madame Indigo but the woman refused them.

'Alan wants you to buy a coat with that money. You'll catch your death walking around in that raggedy thing'.

Maybe death gave Alan the time to think about what he'd denied her, the little television she wanted in the kitchen to keep her company when she cooked, a fluffy bathrobe and a real feather pillow. Philomena fairly skipped out the door in spite of her arthritic left knee. The winter sun, bright though not warm made her feel so much better. A good sign to have light on a winter's day.

The fish was crispy, done just the way she liked it. Ed gave her extra tartar sauce and put the ketchup bottle on the table but she pushed it away. She salted her chips and licked the salt off the ends of her fingers. Madame Indigo was right. She needed a new coat.

When she returned home, there was a mailbox filled with mail but no package from Maeve. She dropped the mail in the metal basket on the table and then retrieved an envelope with a large T for Transamerica Insurance on it. When she opened it, it looked like a life insurance policy. She called the number in the top right corner.

'May I help you?'

She told the man her situation, read off the long number she found on top of the page.

'Please hold, Ma'am'.

It seemed like an eternity listening to canned Beatles music before he came back.

'Philomena Montague? Is there a Maeve Montague?'

'Well, she's Maeve Richardson now. But yes, we have a daughter Maeve'.

Notarised documents would be needed to make her claim; he'd send a packet.

When Philomena hung up the phone, she put on her old coat, imagining the soft coat she would buy, camelhair, calf-length. She grabbed her car keys and headed out the door to tell Madame Indigo about this sudden turn of fortune. A light snow was just beginning to fall, coating the trees with tiny crystals. She touched one that fell on her sleeve, tentatively brought it to her lips and it tasted exactly like the sugar she sprinkled atop Christmas cookies. Snow was coating the roads, and her old car slid over to the other lane before she pulled it back. She couldn't remember whether you were supposed to steer toward the skid or away, so she tapped the brakes and slowed to a crawl, pulling into the first space on West Main Street.

Psychic Journeys was right across from Ed's Diner. No, across from Ed's Diner was The Rainbow Café. Maybe it was down the street a little farther. Which way did she turn when she put the forty dollars back in the envelope and walked across to Ed's Diner? Philomena walked up and down West Main Street. Finally she headed back to her car and went home to tell Maeve about the insurance money. Floating. Yes, she was quite sure Madame Indigo said it was like floating.

On Wednesday the packet arrived and she went to have the paperwork notarised at the Eastside Savings and Loan. When she walked by The Rainbow Café, a scattering of stars decorated the window above a violet door with a pink tassel hanging from the window shade. A nice tea and perhaps something sweet would be lovely. The door chime sounded tinkling bells like the ones she once heard in a monastery. When the tattooed man pressed the change into her hand she noticed a keychain with a crystal ball hanging by the cash register. Philomena lingered at the pastry case, marvelling over perfectly-shaped tarts and scones. She should bake another pie for Mrs Prendergast and Christophe.

A nice apple or pumpkin pie.

Small lacquered tables with rainbows and little stars painted on them ringed larger tables. Snow piled up outside and the place began to fill up with mothers and children in down parkas that made them look like colourful little snowmen. So unflattering, Philomena thought. Then a green-caped woman in a jewelled hat moved her bulk ahead in the queue, ordering a chocolate croissant and hot cocoa *with extra whipped cream.* Philomena waved both hands.

'Madame Indigo. Madame Indigo!' The woman ignored her, quickly swallowed up by a group of ice hockey players with sticks and jackets, laughing and pushing in the queue that now reached to the door. Philomena had been daydreaming about Alan, how they always said they'd return to Florida, rent a place with hibiscus blossoms and pink tile, maybe take Little Robbie to Disneyworld. Yes. Little Robbie's winter break was coming and that is what she'd do. She could see his smile and those dimples, *deep as craters*, Alan used to say. The door chime tinkled again and Philomena thought of *It's a Wonderful Life* and Zuzu who said that every time a bell rings, an angel gets his wings. Now that Alan was dead, she thought of him sitting on a cloud that looked like the froth on a cappuccino, his feet in those ugly plastic sandals he wore with socks. She missed flying, clouds below and blue sky, bright as Little Robbie's eyes. After Alan retired, there wasn't enough money for vacations. *Every day is like a Saturday, Phily* he told her but it didn't feel like it when even going to a movie was too expensive. When she looked back at the queue, Madame Indigo had disappeared, along with the hockey players. A few groups of women sat at the tables, and she picked one near the door, in case Madame Indigo returned.

Philomena opened her voluminous black handbag, took out the manila envelope that would need to be posted today. *Certified mail*, the notary told her. Maeve had been nagging her to take a class in managing her finances and there was one at the Senior Centre. Yes, she'd sign up once she had the insurance money.

'Your hat, Ma'am'.

The same young man from the register with a Chinese tattoo that looked like a pinwheel presented an enormous felt hat with an asymmetrical jewel on it, along with her cup of Oolong tea and raspberry muffin. When he pivoted, Philomena glimpsed his red pointy shoes, etched with leaves and flowers.

'Wait, mister, sir. This isn't mine'.

'But you laid it on the counter Ma'am', the young man said. He had a slight accent like someone from an island who might drink a sweet drink out of a coconut. The young were not as polite as they used to be. Maeve was never like that. She knew to say *excuse me* and *thank you* and little Robbie was learning this as well.

'The owner was in here a few minutes ago, in the queue. I lost her when the ice hockey players came in', Philomena motioned to the tables, now empty.

'Ice hockey players?' The young man raised his eyebrows and repeated, 'I saw you put it down on the counter'.

'You must be mistaken. I'll take it though. I'm sure I can locate the owner'.

The hat was heavier than she expected, some sort of tightly wrought wool but soft, like fur. To tell the truth, the off-centre jewel unsettled her like shoes on the wrong feet or a manufacturer's tag sticking out of someone's blouse. Nothing seemed to be right, snow obstructing her view of the street, the café suddenly empty, and the rude man briskly walking away on pointy red shoes that belonged to someone else.

IT'S UP TO YOU, NEW YORK

I never let work interfere with living, my father often said.

Children shouldn't be seen or heard, Uncle Bimmy said last week.

Uncle Bimmy lived with us, if you call where we live, behind a chain link fence next to an abandoned factory, an actual place. *Our encampment,* Dad called it. We had a little stove made from Budweiser cans, and black plastic trash bags with duct tape stretched over a wooden frame kept us dry. Uncle Bimmy, Dad, and this guy with three teeth, Donald, built *our abode* from scraps they found at the dump. My mother left after a week. *Not for me,* she said before she got into a Chevy Impala with Lenore thirteen months ago. On the really cold days, we went to the St Augustine Shelter, which had a section for women with hot showers and flush toilets. It smelled like body odour and Pine Sol.

When Mrs Shemansky asked me to invite my parents to The Honours Club Awards Dinner, I told her that my mother was dead and my father was on medication and couldn't drive. Last year I told Mr Heffenbacher that my father had moved to Brazil and I lived with my Uncle Bimmy who worked all the time. I didn't mention that Uncle Bimmy stole Sue Grafton mysteries from the town library and chewed tobacco so his teeth were all brown. On cold days, Uncle Bimmy read mysteries by the stove while Dad went to the community centre to sell stuff on eBay. That's how we bought food. Other times he went dumpster diving in the restaurant district by Prospect and West Main Street.

'Perfectly good head of lettuce. Look at this loaf of French bread, still in the paper bag. Americans are so wasteful'.

I ate mostly at school or at Burt's house. Burt didn't ask questions. When I had girlfriends, it was different.

'Let's go shopping, Mandy. You need new clothes', Elaine grabbed my arm.

'I have to go home and help my mother paint the baby's room today'.

I had told her my mother was pregnant and sick a lot.

Guys never asked to go to the mall. They'd rather hang out. I told them I was a lesbian so they didn't bother me. Burt liked to watch old movies downstairs in his knotty pine and stucco family room. No one was ever home at his house and the refrigerator was stocked with cheese, ham, apples and milk. We made ourselves overstuffed sandwiches and watched *Mr Smith Goes to Washington* and *Adam's Rib* with Katherine Hepburn and Spencer Tracy. If I wanted another sandwich, I just went and made one. Their cheese was in a huge block. Sometimes they had sliced turkey or roast beef in little paper packages. He said no one cared if we ate it all because his stepmother went to the market most days on her way home from work. I imagined her with blonde hair dyed lighter than Burt's sandy tangle, a business suit and heels, grocery cart bumping along, filled with adorable packages of deli meats, mayonnaise, pickles, unadulterated lettuce, and maybe some peaches or cherries, off-season. Once we ate an entire bag of Rainier cherries, sitting in plastic chairs on his porch. We spit out the stones, hitting Beanie, his Yorkshire terrier a few times.

Where I lived, I only had a sleeping bag and an upside-down crate served as a table. My books were stowed in a canvas shopping bag with a zippered front pouch from Super Big Lot. It was better if I wrapped it in plastic at night because we got leaks sometimes. I had a flashlight and a headlamp, a gift from my mother before she left.

'You can come with us, you know, Mandy'.

Lenore nodded, her cow-like teeth smiling at me. She had a big hairy mole on her left cheek and a habit of scratching herself. Lice, I thought. I didn't think I could look at that mole for any length of time. Besides, my mother was a cocktail waitress who had, more than once, brought home some loser. I didn't need an unrelated man with a sixth-grade education bossing me around. Dad and Uncle Bimmy didn't bother me. They were too busy trying to avoid any type of gainful employment.

After two months of going over to Burt's house every day, I finally asked if I could take a shower. He raised one eyebrow, which made him look a little like Spencer Tracy and directed with his thumb toward the bathroom with the Van Gogh *Starry Night* shower curtain and stacks of plush pink and blue towels. Last month, he offered the washing machine and dryer. Now every Thursday, I brought a little bag of clothes and threw them in the Whirlpool. Sometimes he added in a few things from his sister's closet. Away at college, she left lots of clothes behind. *She doesn't even use this stuff. Take what you want.* I found her stash of tampons and sanitary napkins so I didn't have to go to the nurse, pretending I forgot them. In the back of her closet, there was a pair of real leather boots that fit if I wore two pairs of socks.

In late October, Burt suggested New York.

'Let's get the hell out of this boring town. We could see a show, go to the Metropolitan Museum of Art, and stay overnight at the Y'.

I told Dad I had a school trip.

'How are you going to pay for it? Trips cost money. I remember, Amanda'.

He didn't remember much.

'I've been returning bottles'.

Returning bottles was respected in my family. Uncle Bimmy did it most days. He also sat on the corner of Spruce and Main in his old army uniform with a coffee can that said *Disabled Vet* on it. Dad said Uncle Bimmy spent his army time playing oboe in an army band in Omaha, Nebraska.

'Why don't you stay over this Thursday and we'll go to New York Friday since there's no school?'

'What about your parents?'

I couldn't imagine anyone's parents letting a homeless seventeen year-old girl stay with their son, even one who said she was a lesbian. I sort of imagined that Burt didn't have parents. The refrigerator was always full like a fairytale where when you ate something, it was magically replenished the next day. For some reason, he didn't appear to appreciate this charmed life. Whenever I asked him about his folks, he shrugged.

'Necessary evil'.

His face crinkled up into a crooked Burt-style smile.

'You can stay in Sheila's room'.

We were both in honours classes, hoping the better schools would make us offers and we could start our real lives. I couldn't wait for room and board, a chest of drawers and a shared bathroom with hot water and a soap dispenser.

This had been a particularly nasty autumn. The cold rain made everything smell like mildew. I'd given up on trying to keep anything but my schoolbooks dry.

Staying in his sister's clean room with bookcases, windows framed by polka dot ruffled curtains, and a desktop computer with internet access was hard to pass up.

'Ok. If you're sure'.

I picked out an outfit to wear to school that wasn't one of the ones pilfered from Sheila. I had visited St Joseph's charity free store last week to stock up on sweaters and to find a raincoat. Burt got an allowance of $20 a week plus he worked at Feeney's Hardware some weekends.

'Weekend's on me'. He handed me an envelope with cash and my bus ticket.

I had put my clothes in the Super Big Lot bag and put that in a plastic bag. The kind of rain that turns the sky black and angry and streets into rivulets was falling so we ran most of the way from the bus stop. I smelled the wet sheep smell of my drenched wool sweater. We dumped our raincoats in what Burt called a mudroom, a little space off the garage where there was a collection of shoes and boots, jackets and umbrellas. Burt handed me a plush towel.

'Your hair is sticking up', Burt hugged himself, he was laughing so hard. 'You look like Charlize Theron in *Monster*'.

I felt the top of my head and sure enough, my reddish-blonde hair was wadded in a wet ball. I'd knotted it and tied it with a piece of twine I found by the picnic table at our camp this morning. Still, there are worse things than looking like Charlize Theron, even made up to look plain and psycho.

I ducked into the bathroom for a shower and a sampling of products like chamomile and aloe hair conditioner and lavender soap. When the garage door opened, I was soaping up my hair for the second time, the pulse of the warm water from the massage showerhead loosening the knots in my back. Then the side door slammed. It wasn't until I turned off the shower that I heard her yelling.

'What's this pile of shit down here?'

Another door slam.

'Are you deliberately trying to piss me off?'

Shuffling and the opening and shutting of drawers.

I strained to hear Burt's low voice.

'Yeah. She's here. Sorry, Angela. *Miss Angela*. I'll clean it up right away'.

I recited French conjugations and my vocabulary words *une veste, un blouson, un chandail*, then ran the faucet a few times. The towels were mostly pink or blue even though the bathroom was painted light green. I opened the medicine cabinet and looked at bottles of Bayer aspirin, Benadryl and cough syrup. There were some bobby pins and barrettes in a little ceramic cup. I combed my hair, fastening a bobby pin on each side so it didn't fall in my eyes. Then I put a thin black line of eyeliner under each eye and a little smudge of glittery purple shadow on my eyelids. Some astringent that smelled like grapefruit tingled when I dabbed it on with a cotton ball so I moisturised with Oil of Olay Facial Rejuvenation. By now it was nearly 5.45 according to the watch Burt had left by the sink. There were cooking smells, chicken and something sweet like pie or cookies.

'Tell me again. Slowly, this time'.

'You look twenty, tops. I'm lucky to live here because if you said the word, he'd kick me out. I promise to do better, *Miss* Angela. I will paint your toenails any colour you want and fold the clothes'.

I want to wake up in the city that never sleeps, Burt sang last week while we were eating leftover chicken parmesan and watching Frank Capra's *You Can't Take it With You*. I'd seen the electronic billboards in Times Square on television, heard about the runners and dog walkers in Central Park. Through the bathroom window, I noticed the weather had cleared and stars were popping out of blackness at intervals like lights on the marquees on Broadway.

The window was small but I'm a wiry girl. I pushed out the screen and dropped my Super Job Lot bag, heavy with feminine products and soap, a towel, and the envelope with the bus ticket and fifty dollars Burt had given me, *in case you lose me or something*. I landed with a thump on a mound of wet dirt, brushed myself off, tiptoed to the back door and unlatched it as quietly as I could, retrieving my raincoat, shoes, and sweater. Under the rutted moon, I headed toward the bus depot where there would be vending machines, coffee and smooth benches, shiny from the backsides of weary travellers.

GOOD HEART

That familiar shuffling sound could only mean one thing. Why didn't he bring the damn rifle, to fire a warning shot? He climbed back in the truck, revved the engine a couple of times, letting out a cloud of exhaust. Then the door to the yellow-shingled shed cracked open and a dirty blonde head emerged. A blonde head attached to the body of what looked like a young woman.

The year before Bessie died, Nick came home to help with the garden. When they opened up the shed, a family of skunks scattered, black and white tails raised, bright eyes menacing. *So cute,* Bessie had said before one of the skunks sprayed Nicky. He had to take a bath in tomato juice and burn his clothes in a fire they built in the backyard. In the early years, Bessie had prayed for another child but the Good Lord only gave them one. *You know our Nicky's wife is pregnant, Bessie. Gonna have a grandbaby. Planting vegetables to bring them like you would've done.* He had imagined her smile and nod of approval.

Bessie's second home, the shed in the back of their house, next to a fenced-in garden that she had faithfully tended. She grew vegetables he'd never heard of like arugula and beets. *You've got to eat better, Ace. It isn't healthy to be having so much meat at your age.* She was right, of course. Sausage, eggs and grits with a pat of butter the size of a billfold were clogging up his heart for sure. Sometimes he thought he felt it seize up like a clenched fist and he'd think he was a goner until it passed and he'd go outside to mow the lawn, rake leaves or pile up mounds of snow with his plough. When *Ace Auto Care* was still open, he didn't think about it much. Too busy trying to keep Joe and Clyde employed when it seemed every car dealer in town offered extended maintenance warrantees. He even came up with the Ace Certificate of Excellence (ACE) and a free oil change with a stamped card of ten paid ones. Bessie suggested coffee and donuts. She ran the desk for him, greeted every customer, and gave them calendars she put together with her photographs of flowers and local farmland. It all went to ruin when she died. Clyde tried to work the computer but a virus wiped out years of accounts. Horace sold the business to Joe two years ago, set about painting the house and refinishing the kitchen cabinets like he had promised Bessie.

Horace jumped down from the tractor, walked over to the skinny figure. As he got closer, he could see caked dirt on her jeans and a filthy t-shirt under her ripped plaid button-down, the air rife with body odour.

'Please don't hurt me'.

'Course I won't hurt you, young lady. What are you doing in my shed?'

Her eyes darted around. Not a cloud or a shade tree in sight.

'Got no place. Thought it wouldn't do any harm to stay here a while, just till I figure things out. Was going to go soon'.

She opened the shed door wider and from where he stood, he could see a greyish sleeping bag on the floor, a loaf of bread and jar of peanut butter on one of the shelves, flashlight, duffle bag, and a photo of a white-haired woman with surprised eyes. The girl pushed her stringy hair out of her face, hiked up her jeans. Bessie had wanted a daughter. *Our Nicky is a good son but I wonder what it would have been like to have a girl. One of my own, you know. Shopping for clothes, talking about boys.*

'That your Momma?' Horace pointed to the photograph.

'Grammy. She lives in Florida'.

'Horace Everly'. Horace stuck out his hand.

'Millie. Millie Benson'. Millie offered her hand, fingernails with half-moons of black at the top.

'Well, Miss Millie. Why don't you hop on the tractor and come back to the big house and clean yourself up. Then you can tell me all about Grammy and what you're planning to do'.

'Sure?'

'Absolutely. A beat up tool shed is no place for a young woman'.

Horace unloaded the hoe, spade, flowers and mulch to make room, patted the burlap sack in the back, and Millie sat cross-legged on a half-filled bag of seed.

'Thanks. I'm pretty dirty. Won't your wife be mad?'

'Wife died three years ago. Just me and Bounty, my collie'.

Millie stared at him for a few seconds then uncrossed her legs, stretching them out and pointing her nearly black sneakered toes. Horace pulled the tractor alongside the back patio and Bounty trotted over with a growl, sniffing and making a rumbling sound in the back of his throat.

'He won't hurt you. C'mon, Bounty. Show your manners'.

Bounty sat on his haunches and scratched behind his ear, then barked at Millie. She put out her hand but he snapped at it.

'Bounty! No!' Horace pointed to the fence and Bounty skulked off.

He held the screen door open, watched Millie take off her sneakers, leave dusty trails across the oak floor.

'Bathroom is the first door on the right. I'll fix you lunch while you clean yourself up. There are women's clothes in the closet in the bedroom on your left. Some might fit you. Might not be your fashion but they're clean'.

Millie ducked into his bedroom and he could hear hangers being pushed over. He felt a little clench in his chest. Finally he heard the bathroom door close and the shower running.

Horace put together a respectable toasted cheese and tomato on rye bread with some leftover potato salad on the side. He heard the bathroom door open and the hangers being moved again in the closet. Finally Millie walked into the kitchen in a green polo shirt and jeans that had belonged to Bessie. The jeans were loose and she had cinched them in with a belt and rolled up the cuffs. Still it was a close fit. Millie's blond streaky hair was combed and pulled back in a ponytail. She had skin so pale that tiny blue veins zigzagged her forehead and the deep shadows under her eyes were prominent as shiners. Her eyebrows were plucked to thin upside down vees making her eyes bulge, almost frog-like. She looked even younger now that she was cleaned up. The lump in his throat made it hard to swallow. Bessie had worn those jeans to AA meetings, and afterwards they went to the pie restaurant. Strawberry rhubarb, her favourite. Once she had dribbled a bit of strawberry on her jeans, dabbed at it with a napkin dipped in water but a faint pink stain was still visible. The polo shirt was for gardening, green like the thick rows of lettuce and squash tops Bessie used to weave in and out of, dragging the sprinkler behind her.

'How old are you?' Horace asked.

'Nineteen', said Millie. 'Twenty in July'.

Horace would have guessed seventeen but girls of that age all looked so young to him. A grandchild on the way, and Bessie would never get to hold the baby in her arms, something she wanted so badly.

You think our Nicky will ever marry? Every Sunday, I pray I'll have a grandbaby.

He'd reassured her that Nick would find someone. Even at thirty. It wasn't too late. Nick called to tell Horace about Portia eight months after Bessie died.

I wish Mother could have met her, is what he said.

Millie ate the sandwich and potato salad in seconds, downed the large glass of milk he put in front of her.

'Want another?' he asked.

She nodded.

'What happened to your wife?' she asked.

'Heart attack. God's will I suppose, but I think it was supposed to be me. My wife, Bessie, took such good care of herself. Had a check-up three weeks before and the doctor said she had perfect numbers – cholesterol, blood pressure. Didn't even eat ice cream though she loved it. Only fifty-eight'.

'Jeez, that's younger than Grammy'.

'I should have remembered the aspirin. You're supposed to give a single baby aspirin to a person having a heart attack'.

'I didn't know that', Millie chewed her sandwich thoughtfully. 'What does it do?'

'Buys time. You know, till the ambulance comes'. Horace's throat tightened and his nose burned. He hadn't talked about this with anyone since he went out with Nicky after the funeral.

'I mean I could've understood breast cancer. My cousin Lynn got it at forty-seven. Can sneak up on a woman of any age. To tell you the truth, I prayed to Jesus, asking that Bessie be spared breast cancer. I should have just asked

Jesus to keep my Bessie alive. It seemed like a mix-up, Bessie dying of a disease that she wasn't supposed to get. Sometimes I wonder if somehow a heavenly wire got crossed and Jesus took Bessie when it was supposed to be me'.

Millie checked the tightness of her ponytail, licked her thumb and picked up leftover crumbs.

Horace plopped another toasted cheese sandwich on her plate, pushed the bowl of potato salad next to it.

'This is really good'.

'Do you want to tell me what happened?' He sat in the chair opposite her.

Millie shook her head. 'Can't talk. Got to go someplace else'.

'How come?'

'Jimmy, my ex, is over in Emeryville. He's really mad at me'.

Horace looked up at the ceiling for a moment. Jesus was telling him something; he only wished he knew what it was. Joe had offered to keep him on after he changed the name to Joe's Auto Care. He tried it for a few months but his heart wasn't in it. People couldn't afford to buy new cars anymore so business had picked up. Every time he looked at the swivel chair in front of the computer, he could see Bessie fiddling with the keyboard, sipping her cup of green tea with the damn antioxidants that didn't do anything to save her.

'Do you want to call your grandmother?' Horace motioned to the phone on the wall.

'Could I?' It sounded more like *Couff-e* since her mouth was full of grilled cheese and tomato.

'Just dial 1 and the area code. We have all distance so it's free'. Horace realised he said 'we' instead of 'I'. The voice mail still had Bessie's voice cheerfully announcing that they couldn't get to the phone right then and to please leave a message. Nick and Portia's baby would be born in August. Hopefully he would have Heirloom tomatoes and kale to bring them. He'd make the seven-hour drive to central Maine talking to Bessie all the way as he did anytime he was in his truck.

'Can you believe our boy really married? And Portia – she's perfect for him don't you think? She really seems to love our Nicky'.

Sometimes he'd put on her favourite music, Bonnie Raitt or Sweet Honey in the Rock. She used to sing along:

Laugh just a little too loud
Stand just a little too close
We stare just a little too long
Maybe they're seein' something we don't, darling.

He could hear her voice, raspy from those years she smoked, before they met, and she gave up alcohol and cigarettes *for Jesus*, she said. *I was just using those addictions to avoid the Lord.* After they met at AA in Emeryville, he knew he could be clean and sober if he had Bessie to wake up to every morning. He reminded himself of that every day since she died, all the times he wanted to reach for a Budweiser or Jack Daniels. It was better when he didn't go out. At first he'd go to Happy Hour at The Thirsty Duck with Clyde and Joe, nurse a ginger ale. Later he wanted that Guinness or Bud so badly, he could feel the gnawing in his belly. After Bessie died, he told them he was busy. The cabinets needed refinishing and the closet still hadn't been cleaned out.

'My son and his wife are expecting a girl. My wife, Bessie, always wanted a daughter'.

Millie smiled a kind of half smile. She had finished the second sandwich and her third serving of potato salad, wiped her hands on the napkin.

'You know you can stay as long as you need to figure things out. Don't need to be in that shed. Got an extra room down the hall'.

Millie shook her head.

'Thanks, but he'd find me here for sure'.

'Well, you think about it. I'll wash up while you call your Grammy'.

Horace handed her the cordless phone.

She perched on the front steps while Horace piled the dishes in the sink. He could hear Bounty scratching his claws on the wooden landing.

'Shoo, doggie. Shoo', Millie said before she moved toward the side of the house.

Horace cracked the door open; afternoon sun bathed the yard in light. At sunset, a pink glow would be visible just at the edge of the hill. He used to take Bessie there, spread a blanket, and they'd eat fruit or cookies, watch the sun drop lower and lower. Once he talked her into making love in the tall grass, though she kept looking around for intruders, complained gnats were biting her bottom.

Millie finally reappeared, her eyes slits of blue though the sun had faded to a slash of light at the edge of a cloud.

'Was your Grammy home?'

'Uh, yeah. Thanks'. She laid the phone back in the empty cradle, sat back down and sipped at the glass of milk Horace had left for her.

'Do you want a piece of fruit or something?'

'Nah. I'm full'.

Millie's leg tapped and bumped against the underside of the table.

'I can give you a ride to the station'.

Then he heard the car, Bounty barking and growling at the same time.

Millie darted into the bedroom and the closet door slid shut.

A stocky man with a crew cut and a backwards baseball cap climbed out of an old Dodge pick-up. Horace locked the door, called 911. It took about six minutes for an experienced burglar to break into a house; he read that somewhere. Six minutes. The Emeryville Police Department was at least fifteen minutes away. The man was close enough to the door pane that Horace could see blackheads around his nose, a little silver ball pierced through his upper lip. He pounded on the window so hard that Horace thought his fist would come right through the glass, yelled something that sounded like *fucking slut*. Horace winced, silently apologised to Bessie. Then he heard the closet door slide open.

Millie walked into the kitchen, his wife's duffle bag slung over her shoulder, Bessie's heart-shaped locket around her neck, and the gold wedding ring with the diamond chip on her finger. She clicked open the deadbolt, fixed her bulging eyes on him.

'Thanks for the sandwich'.

Jimmy leaned toward Millie, whispered something before he pushed her into the passenger seat of the pick-up, Bounty barking up a storm.

'Shut the fuck up', Jimmy yelled out the window before he sped in reverse down the driveway, dust and pebbles flying.

The ache in Horace's temples came on like a hive of bees, louder and louder. Bessie, in her green flowered dress at the county fair, her arm looped through his, the fiddle band playing until midnight, and afterward they walked through the abandoned tents, smelled fried dough and popcorn, and looked up at the crescent moon. He felt a swelling in his chest for all his blessings, all the ways she had saved him by showing him the Lord.

The Cooling

The heat wave grabbed me in its jaws and shook me like I saw the neighbour's dog do once with a rabbit. Even the clothes on the line seemed limp and perpetually damp. Six o'clock and neither of us felt like firing up the grill. I could barely muster the energy to throw together a salad, open a tin of tuna. Don went straight to the fridge, poured himself a cool one.

'Darlin', let's forget supper', his hand around my waist.

If I wasn't self-conscious about the weight I'd gained from the baked goods he constantly brought home, I'd have been butt-naked. I wanted to climb inside that refrigerator, slip into the crisper. The hand on the waist was Don's idea of foreplay. Subtle, I thought. But it had to be done.

I let him lead me into our bedroom, or *boudoir*, as he liked to call it. He'd just come home from work and though he worked in an office, he smelled like a combination of sweat and toner from the copying machines that he repaired. Estelle once told me Michael's scent made her hot. *Sometimes he comes up behind me with that clean man smell when I'm roasting a chicken or whipping potatoes. It makes me want to rip off my skirt right then. You know what I mean?*

I'd nodded as if I understood but I'd never liked the way Don smelled, even fresh from a shower. It was pheromones or something. Unfortunately my scent got a rise out of him every time. Now with it hot as blazes, he steered me toward our brass bed. Thank God I'll never have to do this again.

It was my Nanny Truda, who told me to go with Don quick *before one of the other ladies gets 'im*. Nanny Truda bought me my first sanitary napkins, told me the facts of life, or at least her version of them which was that men have these fat stems between their legs that grown women like pushed inside their private place or woo-woo, which will grow big enough when they're older. Lara Reingold must have grown her private place faster than the rest of us, I thought at the time, since she was pregnant at fourteen. I couldn't imagine enjoying a fat stem of any kind shoved up my woo-woo, but what did I know? It wasn't until Erica Stevens stuck her tongue into my mouth at an eighth grade sleepover that I learned my body could indeed respond.

Don is a good boy, Nanny Truda told me, which meant he had no scandal attached to him yet. Paying job, nice apartment, and at thirty-one, he had never been married.

Damn shame that I'd just changed the sheets, even washed the duvet cover and ironed it. Too hot for covers and I just knew Don would leave a spot. One of his hands probed under my dress, his other hand unhooked my bra, and all I could think of was having to wash the cover again and just when was I going to find the time to iron? It wouldn't lie flat unless it was properly ironed. Don kissed me, sloppy and wet. I turned my face to the side, pretended I had something in my eye.

'Maggie. You're beautiful', he said, as romantic as it gets for Don. It basically meant, get that dress off so I can do ya. I glanced at the neon Budweiser clock he'd bought at the flea market. 6:30. We could be done by 6:45, which would give me time to make the salad, even mince garlic and squeeze a lemon for the dressing. I could tell him over dessert, a vanilla bean gelato I'd bought at the Italian grocer. I rolled over onto my back, eased off the dress and panties, braced for entry. It reminded me of pilots announcing, *prepare for takeoff.*

Thirteen grunting and sweaty moments later, Don rolled off. I had managed to slide the dress underneath me. I have better things to do with my time than laundry, like filling out the W-4 form to send to Whyte and Johnson for my new job as a programmer in Maine. The stench coming off of Don was pungent as a hospital emergency room. *Prepare for landing.* Don smiled at me. 'You're a good woman, Maggie'.

I grabbed another sundress from the closet. In the bathroom, I shoved over his electric razor, that lime-spice cologne that smelled like disinfectant, and an old copy of *Sports Illustrated*. My new bathroom would have a pine chest of drawers, soft pastel towels, verbena and oatmeal soaps, and maybe some bath salts. I'd paint the walls a light green, stencil daisies around the window.

When I emerged, Don had thrown together the tuna salad, cut up cucumbers, tomatoes, and olives, drizzled all of it with olive oil. He'd done a decent job, I had to admit, even opened a bottle of Pinot Grigio because he knows I don't drink beer. Too hot to drink anything but water but I sipped tentatively. Maybe the wine would give me courage.

Outside the clouds clustered together and there was a damp smell to the air. We were definitely in for a whopper of a thunderstorm. After dessert, we moved to the porch, the wind kicking up and small branches snapping off and hitting the screen. A bolt of lightning startled us and we went inside to watch the storm from our picture window. Don put his hand on mine, a gesture that had me worried he would suggest having a baby, buying a house, or even a repeat performance of hump and grunt. He cleared his throat, unbuttoned the top button of his shirt, the one with toner stains on the pocket. I could almost feel steam coming off of him. He increased pressure on my hand.

'We have to talk'.

No kidding.

'I've met someone. Didn't mean for it to happen'.

I snatched my hand back.

'You son-of-a-bitch! What the hell are you talking about?'

'I'm in love, Maggie. I met her at the gym. We want to marry. I'm sorry'.

I should have known something was up when he started working out two nights a week. I liked it because I had book group with my friend Beth on Mondays and choral practice on Thursdays. We were giving each other space to pursue our own interests, something Nanny Truda told me was important.

I pulled myself up straight. How dare he? I was the one offered the perfect job in Portland, Maine, a place I'd always wanted to live. I'd lost my moment. He'd pushed me into the role of the injured and I would remain there. All of our friends would side with me because I was, as he said, *a good woman* who didn't deserve to be dumped by someone like him. I stretched my sundress over my knees, slid to the other side of the corduroy sofa, grabbing the brocade pillow and squashing it to my chest.

Don was doing the thing he does with his lip that I hate, biting it and chewing on it at the same time. Another crack of thunder and a flash. Then the lights went out. I wondered if Miss Buff Gym-Rat liked the stench of copy-machine toner. Maybe she thought it was manly. He had smudges on his white shirts and every week I bleached them while he'd been out shagging that woman. Let Miss Gym-Rat bleach and iron his shirts, wash and hang out his polka dot boxers.

'I'll get the flashlight', Don said, feeling his way though it wasn't all that dark out yet.

'There's nothing I need to see', I said.

'C'mon, Maggie. It's not your fault. You've been good for me. You're a sexy woman and I'm sure you'll meet someone else'.

I didn't want to tell him that I had fallen in love with a town and the idea of an apartment of my own. After college, I moved back in with Nanny until she introduced me to Don. A floral couch and pink dust ruffles on my bed, that's what I coveted most of all.

'Why did we have sex?'

'You looked beautiful, standing there in your sundress. It reminded me of how you looked when we met. You had on a green striped dress and your hair was long, pulled back with a barrette. Little white sandals on your feet. I'm sorry it isn't enough anymore'.

I don't think a man pushing his thing into my woo-woo would ever be enough. Donald Frederick Asher was chewing his bloody lip again and I seriously wanted to punch him in the mouth. The lights flickered and then came back on. A flock of geese honked overhead and the toy poodle next door started yipping. I got a whiff of that fresh air that comes after a summer storm.

Did Don plant kisses on Miss Gym-Rat's face? Maybe the partners of trash haulers and septic tank cleaners got used to rank odours, associated them with love. Not me. I wanted a lover who showered before coming to bed, pulled back the covers.

'I'm moving out the end of the month', I told him. 'I've been offered a job in Maine'.

Don looked at me as if I just made that up. Let him figure out what to do with the apartment, clunky furniture, puke-coloured sofa. Maybe Miss Gym-Rat would help him sort it out. Feather their love nest.

'I was going to give you the furniture. Heather has a furnished house and two kids, Darren and Patricia'.

'I don't care if she has a pet boa constrictor and a McMansion in Yonkers. I'm only taking my clothes, books, and the cedar chest Nanny gave me'.

'What about our lease?'

'You're the one who signed it'.

I stood as erect as I could muster, walked out onto the porch in time to see the bully clouds push off. The cooler air flooded me with relief. My paperwork was winging its way to Maine and fireflies were thwacking their light-filled bodies against the screen.

A kind of electricity coursed through me. When I opened the door, the hair on my arms stood on end, and my sundress billowed and flapped like the sail on a catamaran, skimming over the waves of the Atlantic.

TEN MINUTES

Evan Roman wasn't supposed to be out past seven but at fifteen time was a fluid concept. *Make sure you're home before dark*, his mother had said before Evan wheeled his Diamondback bike out of the garage. On nights with a full moon, it was never completely dark. In other parts of the country, light dominated for hours longer, a fact his sister Beatrice liked to tell him.

California is three hours earlier than Maine. It's only four in the afternoon in LA when Mom makes us come home for dinner.

At 6.35 Evan might have turned back, finishing another ordinary summer evening watching TV or playing video games but Stu had texted him and it was a quick bike ride to his friend's house. The commotion he heard at first seemed to be coming from the shrubbery on the side of the road.

Geraniums and marigolds, bossy red and orange amidst the green tufts of grass completed the beautification project of Pine River. His mother helped to raise money for these plantings that screamed from the roadside like loud scarves that old ladies wore. Then he heard it again, a feral cry, low and persistent. Bobcats had been spotted in the area but this was more like the scream of a baby. When he glimpsed the man behind a row of trimmed hedges, a man with a strange monk-like ring of hair, a man who pulled out a shiny blade, Evan slowed down.

If you don't want to be cut up, Chickie, you'll shut the fuck up.

Half-obscured by a bush with red berries on it, the man's head bobbed up and down. Evan was close enough to see splayed legs, hear grunts, the victim small, a girl or young woman. Evan saw a flash of blue as the monk-haired man moved on top of the woman. Then the pile with pink sneakers didn't stir. He half-expected her to call for her mother. Pink sneakers like the ones Beatrice had when she was little.

Evan pedalled madly down Redmond Avenue toward Plum Drive where Stuart lived, the bicycle an extension of his body, bionic legs propelling him. 6.45 when he glided into Stu's garage, pulled out his cell phone and called Emergency 911. Every muscle ached, sweat drenching his t-shirt and fine black hair that usually crackled with static electricity when he removed his helmet but not today. Today, his hair hung in limp strands around his eyes.

In Stuart's kitchen, he couldn't stop shaking even when Stu's mother put her hand on his shoulder.

'Do you want me to call your mother? How about a glass of iced tea with milk and sugar? I'll make you a nice iced tea, extra sugar'.

Evan couldn't taste anything, little fists of ice clinking against his teeth, the dirt-coloured tea sloshing around in his mouth as if he'd forgotten how to swallow. Stuart just looked at him, shoving his hands into the pockets of his cargo shorts.

When he went down to the station they asked him about the ten minutes.

Why didn't you call immediately?

How to tell them that his hands and legs took on a life of their own, transporting him out of the scene to a place where dinner was in the oven, children played on swing sets and slides, and there was a garage where he would pull in, open a door, and pretend for a moment that he didn't see anything at all. He'd almost convinced himself that the scream was actually one of those bobcats he'd read about in the newspaper, crying out in the early evening for a mate, a feral cat with the kind of sharp teeth and claws that can tear apart its prey. Instead he told them that he didn't know. He forgot he had a phone in his pocket, thought of nothing but pedalling away, the open garage with shovels and rakes hanging on the wall. He saw himself opening the side door and going into the kitchen where Stu would be waiting, probably fixing himself a snack or texting Ella, the girl he liked this week. He thought of the peanut butter cookies in the cookie jar and Stu's mother who wore little glasses that made her eyes look like bug eyes.

The *Pine River Herald* said the victim was seventeen. She wasn't named but *a local teenager called the police*. The police had some leads but advised town residents to keep their children inside after dark. Posters of Deathkiss and Mutant Stranger were yanked from his walls and stuffed into the trash bin and he stopped riding his bike, just stayed home and played World of Warcraft on his computer.

Gradually, the summer wound down. Days grew shorter, and Evan went shopping for school supplies and a new backpack. His mother told him to put this behind him. The *Herald* said that the victim had been hospitalised for four days. Contusions and *internal trauma*. He'd told them about the blue shirt, the monk-like balding head. No suspects. Empty streets during the day. Beatrice wasn't allowed out unless she was with their parents. When he did see someone, he or she would nod a head. It seemed as if no one talked anymore. Stu broke up with Ella and Jennifer's parents wouldn't let her out, even to go to the mall in a group. It was August and Evan couldn't wait for school to start.

'Do you think they'll get the guy?' Stu asked him.

'I hope so'.

'Hey, dude. Why didn't you call from your iPhone? I mean you might have been able to stop it'.

Evan decided not to try out for basketball. Throwing an orange ball into a hoop seemed pointless, and wearing a team shirt in the school colours of red and gold was for kids.

In November, they had a suspect, picked up on a traffic violation. Forty-six-years-old, married, with three children. The case would drag on through the winter with subpoenas and court appearances.

Smaller than he imagined, she was flanked by her parents, a petite dark-haired mother and a grey-haired distinguished-looking father with hard, sad creases around his mouth. Evan heard that she was being home-schooled for her final year. She didn't do anything except point to the suspect, the man Evan might have saved her from, pulling her out from behind the bush and lifting her securely onto his handlebars as he sped down the roadway, feet on fire.

When it moved to the sentencing phase, Evan was excused from further appearances. He joined science club and stayed after school, but dropped it when someone asked him:

Did you see him sticking it in?

He shoved Caden McNamara, was suspended in December for punching someone in the lunchroom. His grades went down and college seemed pointless.

'I've got to get out of here', he told Stu, but Stu wasn't listening. Stu hung out with Brendan now. They played

World of Warcraft and were fixing up a mini bike, Beatrice told him.

'Your friends are trying to understand. You have to give them a chance, Evan. None of us know how we'd react in an emergency. You're too hard on yourself. Did you ever think that you might have gotten hurt if you'd intervened?

'No, Mom. I don't ever think that'.

Evan decided he'd join the Navy when he finished high school. See the world. Live among men. In the winter, he could usually count on money from shovelling driveways but no one was hiring. When he stopped at Jake's Java for coffee, people seemed to get quiet. *Yeah, that's him*, he thought he heard someone say before the little bell on the door rang and one of his classmates, Astrid Heidl entered to get coffee and a cruller.

'Hi Evan'.

'Hi'.

'Did you finish *To Kill a Mockingbird*? I thought it was pretty good'.

Evan nodded although the book never left his backpack. Astrid looked down at her shoes, some kind of fancy boots. Her baggy pink shirt hung over her jeans, chest obstructed by a large canvas bag overflowing with books.

'Well, see you in class'.

Evan nodded again.

Lindsey Monahan was her name and she had wanted to be a neurologist, kind of a science genius, Beatrice said. Tiny with bright eyes, her cropped brown hair had fallen across her face in the courtroom, and she held her mother's hand the whole time. Her father's face was wrinkled like he was about to cry. Evan's feet had pumped him away, around and around, down a street he'd been riding on since he was six. He arrived at Stu's, rank and animal smelling. Sometimes screams awakened him at night. He'd hear moans when he started driving lessons, creaks from the wind in the trees or something else.

The Junior Prom was coming up.

Girls brought in printouts of the dresses they wanted, pored over them in study hall. Plunging necklines and the round suggestion of breasts.

If you don't want to be cut up, Chickie.

'Why don't you ask Jennifer Hopkins?'

Teens were walking around the neighbourhood again, tank tops and running shorts, flip-flops in fluorescent colours. Beatrice was allowed out, as long as she was with a friend and back before dark. The days were lengthening, marigolds and geraniums raging on the side of the road.

Everyone's mind was on the prom, jewel-coloured dresses and tuxedos. Families planned safe after-prom parties so there wouldn't be any more tragedies like the year Rick Adams got drunk, smashed his parents' Nissan into a tree, killing Amber Whetstone and giving himself a paralyzing neck injury.

After English class, Evan asked Astrid Heidl to the prom. She was smart, spoke with a lisp and had a sprinkling of pimples around her nose.

'Yes. Thank you, Evan', she smiled, showing small even teeth.

He went to Gentlemen's Attire for a tux fitting, picked out a white cummerbund and a black tie.

Don't you want colour? Here's a nice pink one. Lots of the young men are wearing pink cummerbunds this year'.

No, thank you. I like the white one'.

His mother suggested a red carnation boutonniere but he chose a white one and yellow sweetheart roses with baby's breath for Astrid.

He would ask his mother for extra money to take Astrid to Brindle's Roadside Inn for dinner beforehand. When they stopped at Cut and Style to get his hair cut, he asked his mother if he could get his ear pierced.

'Why?'

'I don't know. A lot of the guys are doing it'.

'Well, I guess it isn't permanent like a tattoo. You can take it out later if you don't like it'.

At Shelly's Bangles and Baubles, they pierced his ear with a device that looked like the hole-puncher he used in school. A sting, and then soreness. He had to clean it three times a day with an antiseptic. He chose a little gold ball.

If you don't want to get cut up, Chickie.

'Nice piercing, man', Stu said. 'Taking Jennifer to the prom?'

'No. Astrid'.

'Astrid Heidl?' Stu wrinkled his nose.

He had to pick up the flowers for the prom tomorrow but tonight he had other plans. *What they lack in fragrance, they make up for in colour* is what his mother said about the geraniums staining the side of the road. He put two bags of rock salt in his backpack, carried the rest, creeping down the roadway and ducking behind hedges whenever the headlights of a car illuminated the road. Finally he found the place, stretched his mother's yellow garden gloves over his fingers and spread a generous amount of salt at the base of each plant. He envisioned the blossoms shrieking, then curling up like the petrified hand of a saint he once saw at a church. After an hour and a half, his fingers ached and his shoulders were sore from hoisting the sacks. It was eight-thirty and completely dark except for the crooked eyebrow of the moon. Time to go home and polish his shoes, buff them with the stiff brush his mother had laid out for him. When he looked down at his feet tomorrow night, he'd see only his reflection as he stomped and pounded his way across the dance floor.

Earthy Top Note

The simple act of studying my hands, sparse hair at the knuckles and a zigzag of a scar from the time I was whittling a giraffe out of curly maple and the blade slipped; that ownership is one of the things I miss. Ducking into Sal's bakery for an almond croissant, the marzipan sweet and rough in my mouth, watching cold drizzle transform the view from our apartment into an impressionist painting, these were modest pleasures. Death also robbed me of mornings with Elena stretching her dancer's body, reaching for her pink chenille robe, only for me to pull her back on the bed before work. I remember her standing in the kitchen in a leotard and tights, sweaty from teaching all those wannabe dancers.

'*Ewww*, Matt. I need a shower', but I'd still get in a long kiss and a moment of feeling her muscular torso pressed up against mine before she pushed me away.

The half-eaten cheddar and mayonnaise sandwich was left no doubt on the counter, spongiest white bread she could buy, pickle with one or two diminutive bites out of it, and a glass of elderberry bubbly, coral lipstick stain on the edge. The organ that saved me before won't help me now. What is a brain once its owner ceases to breathe? That network of neurons and synapses, cerebral cortex all but useless. In ancient Egypt, they used to remove the brain before mummifying the body. Perhaps they reasoned it would only be an obstacle in the afterlife.

Elena left in a hurry after she got the call, yet I remain unable to move or pass through walls, just dust on the butcher-block cart we had bought at a yard sale. I remember how proud she was of the purchase, $30 and only one large scratch down the middle.

'I can sand that out in no time', I had told her.

Two years later, the ugly laceration remained. Elena covered it up with spices and a ceramic utensil holder but I still saw it every time I reached for the basil or minced garlic. A disappointment that gnawed at me until now.

Five years ago, at a pub, Elena looked my way as strangers do when scanning a room. My housemates needed no excuse for a beer, a research paper completed, the home game won or lost. Elena's long dark hair obscured her fine-boned features, pine warbler or goldfinch. Later she confessed she had been watching me while I talked to my friend, probably pushing her hair out of her eyes. Finally I saw her, walked over, holding her gaze long enough to feel a familiar stirring.

'Can I buy you a drink?' A line pulled out of a wallet, passed like currency.

She had observed me unblinkingly, fingers twisting a strand of hair.

'Ok. Strawberry daiquiri, please'.

When Elena's roommate excused herself, I slid onto the faux leather stool at the high table, canned music playing *Love Song*. Elena sipped the girly drink, lipstick kiss on the edge, told me about her performance that weekend in *Calla Lily*. I borrowed a car to get a ticket, attending the first of many performances of Elena bending and leaping in ways that seemed impossible, her body curved and graceful.

Damn it. I can't seem to move at all. I'm invisible, like a game I played as a child, throwing a blanket over my head and scrunching down on the couch until my father snatched it off.

'We're not playing games here, Matthew. Get the hell up and help your mother set the table'.

Formless. Some sort of ectoplasm spread across the butcher block in my own apartment, a penance maybe, to remind me that I could have done something right for Elena just once. I spent what I thought was infinite energy trying to keep her happy, like the time I booked dinner at Chatterley's, had yellow roses delivered to the restaurant. That evening her mother had the first of a series of heart episodes.

'It's Mommy. Mommy's heart. We have to go'.

Date night spent driving to New York only to have the doctor discharge her mother the next day. Our weekend getaway to Block Island last spring started out with brilliant sunshine, a smooth ferry ride, and then a rented moped jaunt from New Shoreham to Crescent Beach until I hit that patch of leaves. Elena sprained her arm and my femur was deemed 'an unfortunate break' by the clinic doctor. *Guess we'll have to take it easy for a while*, I told a teary Elena. *Making shite into roses*, my father would have called it.

Still I was glad I couldn't see the look on her face when she answered the phone. Keys dropped on the table, scrape of the knife inside the mayonnaise jar, and the suck of the gasket when the refrigerator opened and closed. I don't know why I can hear. Death didn't come with a guidebook. Elena put the phone on speaker; a habit I abhorred back when the way she said *I love you, Mommy* at least twice every phone call was enough to send me into the bathroom with earbuds and an iPod.

'Hello'.

'Elena Carillo?'

'Yes. Who's this?'

'Dr Kane. Bradley Hospital'.

'Oh, no. It's Hannah, isn't it? Hannah Wendell'.

Elena's godmother, age eighty-three. Hannah lived two blocks from us and I loved her as much as Elena did. Not only did she tell off-colour jokes, she once told Elena she would have married me if we had met when she was young. I believe I would have loved her right back. Unlike Elena, Hannah rode motorcycles in her youth, spent time in Jordan, Russia and Italy. She worked in a patisserie in Paris for a summer, which is probably how she learned to make the most amazing flaky pastries, and crusty breads that were magically soft inside. Why Elena preferred preservative-laden white bread was a mystery to me.

'No. We need you to come down here right away. Your husband, Matt, has been in an accident'.

'Is he ok? What kind of accident?'

The fuckers didn't tell her anything, hospital protocol.

Leney drove there all full of hope that this was just another stupid thing I'd done like denting our new Honda Civic six days after I drove it home from the dealership. Hope was an accessory for Elena, like her wrinkly pink dance slippers or the silver barrettes she left by the bathroom sink.

Already dead, brought to the hospital dead, it was a waste of an ambulance. The Emergency Medical Technicians flanked my body on the gurney; no need for any of their fancy equipment just the phone to call the hospital with a DOA. Dead on arrival. Not technically accurate since death occurred before arrival. They immediately transferred my body to the morgue on the basement level using a special elevator, the attendant joked as the elevator went lower and lower. *Into the pit*, one of them said. I guess the last thing Mrs Jones needed to see on her way to bypass surgery was a dead guy on a stretcher. Especially a dead guy with a boner. Just one of the ways death has a sense of humour.

Elena would have to identify the body. Glad I'll miss that one. I'd done it for my father, feigning grief at the bastard's passing. My mother told me she couldn't do it. *You know I have no stomach for that sort of thing.*

We didn't even have breakfast together this morning because Elena had an early rehearsal, just kissed leaning against the doorjamb before she rushed off. Sorry for dying on you, Elena.

Then I heard a hissing noise that could only be the bad cat, Rufie. I could picture his narrowed eyes. He had an uncanny sense of knowing when I wanted to be alone and choosing that time to stretch his claws on my pant leg, causing pulls in the fabric that Elena had painstakingly pulled through the other side with a little needle. I could hear Rufie padding toward the verboten butcher block as if he knew that the resident of the apartment who most disliked him was helpless. He purred noisily, scratched his claws on one of the forbidden legs. Another hiss and then a snarl. My lack of a body or voice didn't seem to faze him. I imagined his paws stretching closer and closer to whatever I now was, adjacent to the canister of cornmeal, mason jars of flour and sugar, and Elena's assortment of spices. Finally I heard the chirp of a jay at the feeder by the kitchen window and Rufie scurried across the floor to his gingham pillow at the window seat.

I waited for the rattle of the little cover over the peephole on the door, the sound of Elena's buoyant step, her habit of kicking off shoes and sliding her socks across the wide plank floor. Last week I'd taken both of her hands and twirled her around in her stocking feet while the teakettle burbled and steamed.

There are little lies and half-truths couples tell each other like *money doesn't matter* and *I just want you to be happy*. I came from nothing and Elena had never known scarcity. My father forgot the date of our wedding, and my mother was a wreck, biting her nails, orange lipstick staining her teeth. I sold my grandfather's coin collection to buy the engagement and wedding rings, my secret. My mother's grey hair had been dyed a frightful yellow that day, puffed into little curls that crowned her head like one of those ridiculous bathing caps, yet Elena's parents cooed over her as if she were a much-loved relative. Since my father had been fired repeatedly for showing up late or drunk, a foreclosure of our family home was imminent.

I'll pay the back payments. Got a raise. But Pop has to get help, Ma. His drinking is out of control.

Bloody fool to help the man who kicked and punched me hard enough to cause black-and-blue marks for a week. Ten months later they lost the house anyway. By then I had spent $15,000 of the money designated as our down payment on a house. My fault that we still lived in this rundown two-bedroom apartment.

I was going to tell her tonight, had the letter in my suit pocket. I had already called Hannah and she promised to help the cause by convincing Elena that my current job was going nowhere. We'd have a house with a fenced-in pool and patio, have parties with wine and wax-edged cheeses imported from Denmark and France.

'I'm glad we stayed here', Elena told me one rainy Sunday, my head in her warm lap. No palm trees or avocados in our backyard in Providence, just windows overlooking a brown rectangle of grass. Still my buddy Joe told me what a lucky shit I was to snag Elena.

She's amazing, dude. Don't fuck it up.

When she walked down the aisle, I'm not ashamed to say I had tears in my eyes. A vision in her Victorian cream silk dress with the forty-five seed pearl buttons I would undo later that night. Two weeks in Hawaii, a present from her parents. We sat out on the lanai, a pink plumeria blossom tucked behind her ear, talked about children we would someday have.

Silas or Colton for a boy. Juliana for a girl. Or maybe Deirdre.

My buddies never saw me in a Hawaiian shirt with a flower lei. I would have worn a grass skirt if she wanted it. Once she'd slipped her hands inside my swimming trunks when we were out snorkeling. Another time, she pulled off her bikini top underwater so her breasts floated like luminescent shells.

'Race you to the reef'.

I was thinking of pink aureoles as I swam through the clear water. When I caught up to her, she slipped away and the chase began anew. It isn't possible to hold on to a slippery body. All night I caressed her almost translucent skin until we fell asleep tangled together, didn't stir until the peach-rose dawn streamed across our bed. Two years ago or maybe yesterday. I'd almost convinced myself that I could use those days to buy more time, a winter day with the smell of Elena's dill cheese biscuits, pot of spiced tea between us, another morning with legs and thighs intertwined. Graduation, our wedding day, one more look at the photo on my desk of Elena in a pearl-grey dance skirt, reading the letter again, and signing the contract. Imperceptible particles I could no longer touch.

A cruel fucker, death. There were so many *if onlys*. If only I hadn't talked Reg into an espresso, told him I'd run out for *just a minute*. I was hankering for some strong coffee and Reg had reminded me of the Ethiopian Harar espresso they had on Tuesdays at Lovett's, three blocks away. The scent of lilacs drifted in through the office window and I was dizzy with it, my computer screen blurring in front of me. Elena had another rehearsal after work so I planned on working late, *money in the bank* I called it because I could work a half-day on Friday, surprise her with a weekend getaway. I planned to tell her then about the offer I'd received two days ago from a well-funded California start-up. A dream job. *Your education and experience is an excellent match for Innuendo. A generous relocation package, including the down payment on a house would, of course, be included.* Oranges and sunshine. No downstairs neighbours blaring country music every Sunday, smell of sausage wafting up the stairs.

A brisk walk would clear my head. If only the semi driver hadn't run the red light. I had the walk light, sipping from one delectable cup and holding the other; a perfect espresso, fruity undertone with an earthy top note. Suddenly I felt the breath knocked out of me, cups flying. The truck caught me squarely on the left side. Splinters of light fell like tiny snow globes, each one a complete scene: Elena saying *I do* in her husky voice, her tears over the rejection letter from Julliard in the back of the all-night diner, the late night call about my father's death from cirrhosis, awkwardly sipping a Coke at Mom's marriage to Merv six months later, Elena's thighs, eyes, Elena, the six figure salary offer from Innuendo, Elena's small ballerinas twirling on a rented stage.

After sound was swallowed, my eyes fluttered open to a montage of silent screams, bystanders weeping and holding onto each other, someone punching in numbers on a cell phone, Emergency Medical Technicians with wide sad eyes. Like a disaster movie with the sound turned off. When everything darkened, I heard the clank and creak of the gurney, snippets of conversations. I never woke up or felt myself travel crosstown to land as sediment on the butcher block. Hearing and seeing merged into one sense, no body. Wood, air, sand and breath just words. All pain and urgency fled, leaving behind a long patience.

The EMTs and bystanders would make love tonight, if they had partners. Death had that effect. I had done it myself after my father's funeral, a way to prove I still had body and will. Some of them would pray, check their children several times during the night, straightening bed sheets and stroking soft, warm heads. I would lie here waiting for Elena to return because waiting is what the dead are best at. We have all the time in the world.

IMMERSION

She could hear her mum saying, *That, Gwen, is a man of a certain age but dang, he looks good.* Gwendolyn had noticed him right away, not because of his lean build or weathered face, the hallmark of a man who worked outside, but the clear grey of his eyes and the way he rubbed his hands together briskly even though it was August. His clothes wore him like an emblem. No ring. She tucked a grey hair behind her ear and tugged at her cobalt blue swimsuit. *It's ok to show a little skin, Gwendolyn. You won't meet anyone by wearing those high-necked blouses, mannish slacks.*

Gwen pulled in her stomach, lifted her arms as she spread her towel on the hard-packed sand by Lake Warden. She was thinking about the moon's burnish filtered through the old elm, and how it had traced lacy patterns on her belly and thigh last night as she stretched in front of the open window.

One of those endless summer days when a late swim seemed possible, the orange sun ricocheting off the smooth lake vibrating with energy. A group of skinny grandmother types were splashing near the dock, veined hands gripping wood. The Thursday group had arrived around five with a picnic basket, then walked or limped in, kicking chicken bone legs. Once they attempted a synchronised swim, freckled arms linked together in a circle before they collapsed into laughter. At six o'clock, they pulled out sandwiches, Ziploc bags of carrot sticks, peaches and cookies, all washed down with a jug of pink lemonade. By seven, they walked each other to their cars. Gwen reapplied sunscreen, reached for her book and put it down again like she picked up Jack's racing trophies yesterday, wiping the scrim of dust off with a finger before placing them back on the bookshelf next to the photo of the two of them hiking Mt Katahdin.

'Hope your shoulder feels better'.

Car doors slammed and tires clicked on gravel, kicking up dirt like smoke. Two vehicles were left in the parking lot, her red Nissan and a blue Yamaha motorcycle, silver helmet hanging over the handlebar.

His yellow beach towel and stainless steel water bottle left on the beach as he strode toward the water like the last float in a parade, the one everyone anticipated, even as they folded up the metal limbs of their chairs, packed away the snacks. There was a lull, dragonflies conferring in little clumps of iridescent blue. He took his time entering the lake, muscular legs, flat nearly hairless stomach and an ass that she imagined snug on a motorcycle, her arms wrapped around his waist. When she stood up, her hips moved to a beat that irresistibly travelled up her legs to her *core*, the part that her Pilates instructor told her was so important. Little grains of sand stuck to her feet, tickles and pinpricks that washed off as she immersed herself in the bracing water.

After Jack died, she joined a gym, discovered muscles that protested until she made them do her bidding, contorting her body and welcoming the baptism of sweat. Some days, it was the only place she heard conversation, songs from too-loud iPods, people talking about lats and abs and obliques, and the non-verbals like the smiling spiky-haired woman who arrived with a Nordic looking man, moving apart only after they stowed their gym bags in the same cubby. At eight o'clock sharp they were back at the cubby, sipping from identical blue water bottles, making the kind of eye contact that long-term couples understand. The ba-doops of 80s music and the clang of the machines soothed her, like being in an anonymous crowd in a shopping centre, pausing in front of Maytag washing machines or Samsung flat screens, only to have a salesman edge closer, chatty and amicable. Sometimes she'd feign interest in a gadget, ask about its energy rating or picture clarity, then claim she needed time to consider it, would return at a later date.

'What a moon', she said, when she swam alongside him, the bald moon barely visible in the wide-open sky. It would burgeon as the sky darkened, like her belly rounded with Anastasia, grown-up fawn off in the wilds of Malawi with the Peace Corps. The light dappled her hands and arms as she moved, larger than the moon that Jack once traced on her breasts, called her Luna. At first, she dreamt of him regularly, worrying the sateen border on the blanket to shiny shreds. She'd awaken partially, turn to the whisper of what she thought was there but it was only the hard swallow of grief. Her friends had warned her not to marry a man twenty-two years older, *a recipe for widowhood*. But the passion and pull were strong and then there was Anastasia, dark-skinned like her father, with those incongruous green eyes. Tasi wanted to continue her father's work, his compassion for the larger world abruptly halted. A photo of her daughter running through a field of wildflowers rested by her bedside. At first a steady stream of invitations arrived; dinner parties, holiday open houses. After a year, the calls and social engagements slowed and Gwen joined the gym, bought a subscription for one to the symphony.

When the lodestar moon turned pitted amber, the sky released its black drape. Branches of birch and ash trembled slightly, sending a shiver up her arms. Gwen's wrinkled fingers kept reaching through the silky water – reach, pull, reach. The stranger was doing the breaststroke as if he had always been there.

'What's your name?'

'Robin', he said, 'like the bird'.

He came for her as if he knew she walked from room to room, listened to Bach concertos to fill the space. She reached for him like the door of a house with two dinner plates set, two glasses of Cabernet. Hands found gaps in the fabric, remembered what fingers could do to sing the skin alive. Like the sticklebacks and perch wriggling near the rocks, they joined and separated and the lake responded in kind. Scratch of his face, lips on hers, and then fingers, extravagant hands.

Finally he pulled away, ambled ashore on long legs, shedding his suit like a second skin. She looked at his body, now in shadow. Towelled off, he dressed, dangled keys. The moon, a hubcap now, rust-coloured at the edges, followed her flanks and ankles, hands as she picked up her own towel and waited. Grey eyes caught hers for a moment then darted to the empty beach, dark patches of grass framing the path.

'Are you a mermaid?'

A smile tugged at Gwen's mouth.

'Just call me Luna'.

'Ah, a Moon Goddess. I should have known. Well, Miss Luna. I must be off'.

He jiggled the keys and started down the path.

The sudden whine of his Yamaha marked the pebbles and sand of the makeshift road, jarring at first, then fainter. Gwen moved deliberately. Bright enough to see her lone car in the parking lot, the shrill song of katydids and crickets serenaded her as she opened the door.

Gwen stripped off her bathing suit, tossed it in the back seat. For a moment she stood motionless in the night air, letting her skin dry, nipples erect, goose flesh rising on her arms and upper legs. Standing with her shoulders down, the way she had learned, she tightened her muscles, reached up, as if trying to pluck a star from the sky with the tips of her fingers. Animal eyes blinked on and off behind pine and shrub, beacons that tracked her as she sprinted back to the beach, dove, surfaced and dove again into the lake's dark mouth.

LEASH LAWS

I perch in trees, like a squirrel or woodpecker, always looking over people's heads, spotting a bald spot or the flat part where their hat rested too long, warming the owner's ears. It's not like I'm nimbler than the others, just keener in my vision.

No one knows when his or her tree-time will come. Some folks seem to be glued to the earth with sinews underground like electrical wires. They talk to each other in a way that wastes language, not at all how animals communicate. I speak to Serge by humming even though his room is two doors down. He knows my language, came from a deciduous forest in Maine, and once helped a black bear find the just right den for winter. Because he's mostly human, he doesn't need to hibernate. He used to stay at the St Francis Shelter when the snows came. Like me, he dislikes human food except for berries and nuts, an occasional bird. Carol brings me granola in a plastic container. Glass is better because it's shiny but the Strongmen won't allow it. They are used to making the rules, even ones that make no sense, like when Carol can visit and how much time I'm allowed in the sunroom where I can watch jays raid the birdfeeder, see the cherry trees shrill into blossom. Carol always tells me I'll be home soon, and I think of my favourite maple tree. I don't wound it like the people who insert a metal tap in the tree's torso, hang a bucket to collect the blood. They don't understand that sap keeps the tree strong. It's important to keep one's fluids to oneself.

'Susan. Time for your pill'.

Eliza is a Strongman even though she's female. She wears their uniform of blue cotton with white whispery shoes. I know she wants to read my dreams so she can understand the language of plants and animals but I don't let her. I've learned how to stick the pill in my left back molar, the one with a cavity. When I go to the loo, I spit it in the toilet and flush, watch it spiral down into the septic system but I worry about fish losing their dreams.

I open my mouth like a good robot. Eliza put me on Step Five because I'm one of the well-behaved ones. I don't tie my sheets into knots or spit out mashed potatoes. As long as I can have some nuts and berries, I am quiet as a snake. It is April and soon they'll open up the courtyard. Carol can take me outside and maybe through the gate to Keeper's Park down the street. You have to be a Six to go there but all it takes is opening my mouth and sitting in the semi-circle when Strongman Dr Benton comes in.

'Click, clack, click. How do you feel about that, Susan?'

'Click, clack, clack. I feel fine, Dr Benton'.

There's a dogwood sapling outside the window that has been trying to get my attention. She shakes her greening limbs and tells me stories about the vole that lives underground. I promise to save her some water from the pink plastic pitcher by my bed so her buds will open like promises.

Carol joined the human race at seven. She was never one of us, but it's safer that way. She speaks their language so they let me go places with her. They punch in a series of numbers on the little metal door and then more numbers on the bigger door until it opens to the land of unfenced trees and boxy houses.

'My mother needs fresh air. Do you think I could take her to the park on Saturday?'

'Click, clack, click. Group goals, individual goals, Step Five'.

'Great. I know she'll make Six by then. She's so pale, it will be good for her to get outside'.

Kurt spoke that language, too. He kicked me out early. At first it felt dark and strange because I didn't fit into his forest, buried my roots beyond the park, next to the hiking trail where Carol got lost one day.

'Susan, why weren't you keeping an eye on her?'

Kurt had a kind face, promised to keep me safe when we met on the bench at Creeley Park. I told him about clear cutting, how they were mowing down my relatives with chainsaws, and he laughed, called me an environmentalist, a *treehugger*. He couldn't see the depth of the cuts, the muscles, and all those severed limbs strewn by the path.

'I love how you're passionate about this, Susan. I've met so many people who don't care about the earth'.

I married him because he promised there would be flowers and a trip to see the redwoods in Oregon. We had pink petunias and blue and yellow pansies in ceramic pots so we could plant them outside Kurt's house later. He built me a little wooden bench in the garden, just like the one in the park.

'You can watch your roses and columbine now. You're a funny woman, Susan'.

Then he thought I wasn't funny anymore, sometime after Carol was born. Babies can understand all languages. That's why they don't talk; they're too busy listening. Once they start to speak, they become self-absorbed like the rest of the humans. Their words start to click and clack, and they talk about weather and what kind of poison is best for getting rid of dandelions and ants. I wanted to keep Carol away from all that but Kurt took her from me, put her in a red rectangular building with painted handprints on the wall, and other children who brought their lunches in plastic boxes, didn't understand what the trees and dogs had to say.

Kurt doesn't visit me anymore. He married Adrienne and they moved from the deciduous forest to a place called Stamford. Everything is oblong and grey there. Carol calls it *the city*. She's grown, lives with Seymour, her Irish setter. When I'm on Step Six, the Strongmen will let her bring Seymour to visit me and we can talk about where he's digging and what the earth smells like in April after a rain. Dogs like to talk about smells since their noses are so close to the ground. If allowed to roam, they reminisce about all the animals that have wandered in their path and I feel less lonely listening to them. Kurt thought that barking was the dog just taking a breath, a sharp exhale of air but barking is conversation, a complicated social network that dogs develop to expand the confines of their yards and homes. Sometimes they escape, arrange to meet by the river or down the street, warn each other about the dreaded animal control officer with his green truck. Leash laws are incarceration for canines. I want to destroy all the leashes and short-circuit the invisible fences.

'I have to get an invisible fence for Seymour. They have a leash law in New Fordham now. A little boy was bitten by a Pit Bull and now everyone has to restrain their dogs. I know how you hate that, Mother'.

Pit Bulls are angry that people fear them. They don't want to argue or bite. Little boys and girls tease dogs because they weren't taught to respect animals, and a Pit Bull is like a wrestler. Broadchested and muscular, they don't have to put up with anything. Some days I wish I had more Pit Bull in me.